The Legacy Series Book 1

The Girl in Smoke

A.L. Wilder

Copyright

Copyright © 2026 by A.L. Wilder

All rights reserved.

This is a work of fiction. Names, characters, places, events, and incidents are either the product of the author's imagination or used fictitiously. Any resemblance to actual persons, living or dead, businesses, institutions, events, or locales is entirely coincidental.

Published by
A.L. Wilder Publishing

Second Edition
2026

ISBN: 979-8-9995874-4-2

Other Works by A.L. Wilder

The Legacy Series:

Book 1- The Girl in Smoke

Book 2- Forged in Her Fire

Book 3- Crowned in Her Flame

The Body Trail

Ruin Me Softly

No More

Dedication

For the ones who were told they were too much.
Too strange. Too loud. Too different.

For the ones who were locked in rooms meant to break them.

And for the ones who walked out of those rooms
with fire in their lungs and smoke in their bones.

You were never the monster in their story.
You were the miracle they were too afraid to understand.

Trigger Warnings

This book contains mature and potentially distressing themes. Reader discretion is advised.

This novel includes references to or depictions of:

- Child abuse (physical, emotional, and psychological)
- Religious abuse and spiritual manipulation
- Homophobia and condemnation of queer identity
- Child confinement and imprisonment
- Domestic violence
- Trauma and post-traumatic stress
- Abandonment and parental rejection
- Religious extremism
- Forced punishment using scripture
- Animal imagery and infestations (rats)
- Psychological torment
- Revenge and vigilante-style justice
- Graphic depictions of suffering during magical punishment
- Body horror and supernatural transformation
- Curses and dark magic

- Themes of persecution and persecution trauma

- Mental deterioration

- References to torture

- Supernatural violence

The story also contains:

- Sapphic romance

- Polyamorous romantic relationship

- Dark fantasy themes involving morality, justice, and revenge

Readers sensitive to these topics may wish to proceed with caution.

Author's Note

The Girl in Smoke is a story about survival.

It is about the quiet and often invisible damage that happens behind closed doors. It is about the way shame can be weaponized, the way faith can be twisted into fear, and the way silence can be used to control those who are different.

But more than anything, this story is about what happens after survival.

Evelyn's journey is not simply about escaping abuse. It is about reclaiming identity, finding chosen family, and learning that the things people once tried to destroy in us may actually be the very things that make us powerful.

This book contains difficult themes, including religious trauma, abuse, and the experience of being condemned for loving differently. While the story explores darkness, it was written with one purpose in mind:

To remind readers that surviving the fire does not make you broken.

Sometimes it is the fire that reveals who you truly are.

If you see pieces of yourself in Evelyn, I hope you know this:

You were never too much.
You were never the problem.
And the world deserves the truth of who you are.

Thank you for stepping into the smoke with me.

— A.L. Wilder

Chapter One

Under the Big Top

The Girl in the Fog

I don't remember when I started running.

At some point the road disappeared beneath my feet and the forest swallowed me whole. Time unraveled the deeper I went, stretching thin between the trees until it felt meaningless. My lungs burned with every breath, the cold air slicing through my throat as though it carried tiny shards of glass. Bare branches clawed at the sky above me, thin and skeletal against the dull gray clouds while rain drifted down in a steady whisper. It wasn't heavy enough to pour, but it never stopped. Each drop struck my face and neck like a needle.

The world had narrowed to the sound of my boots striking frozen ground and the ragged rhythm of my breathing.

I couldn't tell if I had been running for minutes or hours. My legs moved on instinct now, driven by something deeper than fear— determination to be free. My boots were soaked through, the leather dark with rain and mud. Cold water seeped through the seams and wrapped around my toes until I could barely feel them. The hem of my skirt clung to my legs, dragging behind me like wet moss as fog crept slowly across the forest floor.

At first it brushed only my ankles, cool and ghostlike, but with every step it climbed higher, swirling around my knees and waist until the world beyond a few feet dissolved into pale gray nothing. When I stretched my hand out in front of me, it vanished inside the mist.

Branches tore at my sleeves and scratched across my arms, leaving burning lines across my skin. I barely noticed. The sting helped. It reminded me I was still moving. Still breathing. Still not in that house anymore.

That house with its locked doors and watchful windows.

That house where silence was expected and questions were treated like sin.

Where love was something spoken from the pulpit but never given freely.

A hollow cry echoed somewhere in the distance, rising through the trees in a long, mournful wail. Maybe it was a wolf. Maybe it was the wind twisting through the empty branches. Or maybe the sound had come from my own chest without me realizing.

My mother's voice still followed me through the woods, sharp and unyielding, as if the forest itself had memorized her words.

The world is a den of temptation, Evelyn.

Her voice lived in my head the way scripture lived in church walls.

A girl like you won't survive a single day out there.

I stumbled over a root and caught myself against the trunk of a tree before I could fall. The bark scraped against my palms as I steadied myself, my breath tearing through my chest.

She was right about one thing.

I wasn't a girl like the others.

And that was exactly why I had to leave.

My journal rested in the hidden pocket sewn into the lining of my dress. I could feel its weight pressed against my ribs with every breath, steady and familiar. The leather cover had softened over years of being opened and closed, its pages filled with thoughts I had never dared to speak aloud.

It was the only piece of my life I had taken with me.

That—and the fire humming faintly beneath my skin.

The sensation had returned sometime during my escape. At first I thought it was only the cold or the rush of blood through my fingers, but it was stronger now. My palms tingled, heat blooming beneath the skin like a hidden coal slowly being fanned back to life. It wasn't painful, but it wasn't comfortable either. The warmth pulsed in slow waves, as though something inside me was waking.

Something restless.

Something alive.

I curled my fingers into tight fists.

Not here.

Not now.

Not where the forest could see.

I don't remember falling.

Only the moment my knees struck the ground. Mud swallowed them instantly, cold and soft as it soaked through the fabric of my skirt. My hands slid forward into the wet earth, and the impact knocked the breath from my lungs in a sharp, humiliating gasp.

For a moment I stayed there bent over in the mud, damp strands of hair hanging across my face while the forest breathed slowly around me. Wind moved through the trees, stirring the fog in long drifting currents while rain tapped against the branches above like soft fingers drumming against glass.

My body trembled with exhaustion.

And something else.

Something building quietly inside my chest.

Then I heard it.

Music.

At first it was so faint I thought my mind might finally be unraveling after hours of running. But the sound returned, drifting softly through the fog.

A calliope wheezed out a slow, melancholy tune. Beneath it, a violin threaded through the melody, its notes rising and falling like a voice trying not to cry. Somewhere behind both instruments, a woman was singing. The language was unfamiliar, the words curling through the mist in a rhythm that made the hairs along my arms rise.

The music didn't belong in the forest.

It didn't belong anywhere near me.

And yet something in my chest leaned toward it.

I lifted my head.

The trees ahead were beginning to thin.

One step.

Then another.

And suddenly the forest opened.

The ground widened into a clearing where fog pooled low across the grass like spilled milk. At the center of it stood a cluster of enormous tents rising from the mist like dark flowers blooming in winter. Red and black stripes spiraled upward along the canvas while lanterns hung from iron posts hammered into the earth, their flames dancing behind glass cages. Warm light spilled through the fog, casting long shadows that moved across the damp ground like living things.

The air smelled different here.

Wood smoke.

Sweet caramel.

And something I could not quite identify.

A weathered wooden sign creaked slowly overhead as the wind nudged it back and forth.

Cirque de Lune Noire.

The carved letters were worn smooth, as if countless hands had traced them over the years.

I stood at the edge of the clearing, rain dripping from my sleeves, staring at the impossible sight before me. Somewhere behind me the forest had vanished completely, swallowed by fog and distance and the life I had just abandoned.

Something stirred quietly inside my chest.

Not fear.

Not excitement.

Recognition.

As if some hidden part of me had always known this place existed.

My foot stepped forward without asking permission.

The moment I crossed into the clearing, the air shifted. The biting cold faded slightly, replaced by a strange warmth that curled through the fog like the breath from a nearby fire. The scent of sugar grew stronger, mingling with perfume and smoke while the music swelled around me.

My heart began to beat in time with it.

"Welcome, darling."

The voice came from behind me.

I spun around so quickly my boots slid across the wet grass. She stood near the entrance of the largest tent, half hidden inside a pocket of shadow that didn't seem to belong to the night around it. Her coat swept to the ground in a spill of black fabric trimmed with crimson velvet while dark curls fell over one shoulder, catching faint glimmers of lantern light.

In one hand she held a slender black cane she didn't appear to need.

Her golden eyes watched me with quiet interest.

Not the curiosity someone might give a stranger.

The patience of someone who had been expecting me.

"You're… the ringmaster?" I asked, my voice barely louder than the rain.

Her lips curved into a slow smile.

"Some call me that," she said smoothly. "Others have chosen less flattering titles."

The fog curled around her boots as though it had been waiting for her.

I glanced nervously toward the forest behind me. "I didn't mean to trespass," I said quickly. "I was just—"

"Running."

She stepped closer, her voice soft but certain.

"From something," she continued thoughtfully, "or toward something?"

"I don't know," I admitted.

Her head tilted slightly as she studied my face.

"You're not lost, Evelyn," she said.

"You're simply late."

My breath caught.

"How do you know my name?"

She didn't answer.

Instead, she extended her hand toward me.

Not for a greeting.

For a choice.

I turned once more toward the forest.

There was nothing left there.

No road.

No house.

No life waiting for me behind those trees.

Only fog.

Slowly, I placed my hand in hers.

Heat surged up my arm the moment our fingers touched.

Not painful.

Not gentle.

Alive.

The corner of her mouth lifted slightly.

"Come," she said.

"The others are eager to meet you."

She guided me toward the towering tent, the canvas shifting in the wind while shadows moved across its surface like restless spirits beneath the fabric. Inside, light and darkness danced together in slow, hypnotic patterns.

I smelled sugar melting over flame.

Heard whispers woven beneath the music.

And deep inside my chest, the ember that had slept there my entire life stirred.

Not weak.

Not frightened.

Awake.

For the first time in my life, the tight knot inside my chest began to loosen.

I was no longer standing outside the world.

I had stepped into it.

And somewhere within the strange, breathing heart of the circus, something was waiting for me.

Chapter Two

Before the Circus

The First Time She Burned

I was twelve the first time I lit a flame without a match.

Winter had settled deep into the bones of the house that year. Cold crept through every crack in the walls and settled into the floorboards until even the air felt brittle. Frost crawled across the inside of the windows in delicate white patterns, turning the glass opaque around the edges like lace made of ice.

My breath fogged in front of me as I knelt on the kitchen floor, scrubbing the wood with a stiff brush.

The water in the bucket beside me had long since turned gray. Lye burned the cracks in my fingers where the skin had split open from the cold, each sting sharp enough to make my eyes water. Every time I dipped the brush back into the bucket, the smell rose up harsh and chemical, scraping the inside of my nose.

Mother stood in the doorway behind me.

She always watched when I worked.

Her arms were folded tightly across her chest, the heavy crucifix around her neck resting against the dark fabric of her dress. The chain shifted softly every time she moved, the faint clink of metal against metal marking each small motion like a warning.

"Elbows down," she said.

I straightened slightly.

"Back straight."

I adjusted again, forcing my shoulders upright even though they ached from kneeling.

"Do it properly, Evelyn. God sees even the smallest laziness."

The brush scraped across the floorboards in slow circles.

I had been kneeling there for what felt like hours.

"Honor thy father and thy mother," I recited quietly.

The words came automatically. Scripture lived inside my head the way songs lived inside other children's. I knew hundreds of verses by heart. Sometimes I wondered if I could still hear my own thoughts beneath all the scripture.

The brush scraped again.

"That thy days may be long upon the land…"

I hesitated, searching for the exact phrasing of the next line.

The slap came fast.

Mother's hand struck the back of my head, sending my forehead dangerously close to the floorboards. Pain flashed through my scalp where her fingers had landed.

"Do not mangle the Word of God," she said sharply. "He hears every syllable."

I swallowed hard and forced myself upright again.

"I'm sorry."

"Again."

I repeated the verse from the beginning, carefully matching the cadence she preferred. Every word had to sound exactly right. Too slow and she accused me of mocking the scripture. Too fast and she said I lacked proper reverence.

There was no correct way.

There was only endurance.

This was my penance.

Every day there was another task. Another prayer. Another lesson about the darkness Mother believed lived inside me.

She never explained what that darkness was.

Only that I had inherited it.

From "HER."

The mysterious woman Mother spoke of only in bitterness.

Never a name.

Never a face.

Just accusations whispered like curses.

That evening, when the chores were finished and Mother disappeared into the parlor for her nightly prayers, I slipped quietly toward the narrow staircase that led to the attic.

The boards creaked beneath my feet, but I had long since learned where to step to keep them quiet. The attic smelled of dust and old paper. Stacks of brittle hymnals leaned crookedly against one wall, their spines cracked with age. A trunk filled with moth-eaten shawls sat beneath the small circular window, its lid warped from years of damp air.

Everything up there felt forgotten.

Hidden.

Which was exactly why I liked it.

My eyes wandered across the cluttered shelves.

That was when I saw it.

The candle rested inside a shallow wooden box tucked beneath a pile of yellowed sheet music. It was ivory colored and nearly untouched, wrapped with a faded ribbon that had once been pale blue.

Even from across the room I could smell it.

Honeysuckle.

I wasn't sure why I picked it up.

Perhaps it was simply the prettiest thing I had ever held.

Or perhaps something inside me recognized it before my mind did.

I slipped the candle into the pocket of my apron and carried the firewood downstairs.

Later that night, when the house finally fell silent, I placed the candle on the narrow windowsill beside my bed.

The glass felt cold beneath my fingertips. Outside, snow had begun to fall in slow drifting flakes that disappeared into the darkness before they could reach the ground.

I stared at the candle.

I didn't know what I expected to happen.

But something inside me felt restless.

My chest tightened with a strange anticipation I couldn't explain. Slowly, I raised my hand and held my fingers just above the wick.

"Please," I whispered.

The flame appeared instantly.

It sprang to life without smoke or spark, as though it had simply been waiting for permission.

Warm golden light filled the small room, dancing across the walls.

I froze.

My heart began pounding so loudly I was certain someone would hear it downstairs. The flame flickered softly, its glow reflecting in the window glass.

I hadn't struck a match.

I hadn't even touched the wick.

And yet the candle burned.

A small laugh escaped my throat before I could stop it.

The sound felt strange.

Too light.

Too happy.

Then the door burst open.

Mother stood in the doorway, her silhouette filling the frame. The lamplight from the hallway spilled around her, throwing long shadows across the floor. The crucifix around her neck swung slowly as she stepped inside.

Her eyes locked onto the candle.

"What blasphemy is this?"

"I—I didn't mean—"

Her hand struck my cheek before the words could finish leaving my mouth.

The force snapped my head sideways. Pain bloomed hot across my skin as the room tilted.

"Witch," she hissed.

The word hung in the air between us like poison.

"Just like her."

My hand rose instinctively to my cheek.

"Who?" I whispered.

Mother's face twisted with fury.

She crossed the room in two quick steps and knocked the candle from the windowsill. It struck the stone hearth with a sharp crack, the wax splitting as it hit the floor.

The flame vanished instantly.

The room fell back into darkness.

"You think I don't see it?" she said, her voice low and trembling with anger. "The way the world bends around you? The way candles light themselves when you're near?"

Her fingers wrapped suddenly around my chin, forcing my face upward. Her nails bit into my skin.

"It's unnatural," she said.

"And God does not tolerate the unnatural."

I said nothing.

I had learned long ago that speaking rarely made things better.

"You will pray until it is burned out of you," she continued. "You will learn obedience."

Her grip tightened.

"Or God Himself will strike you down."

She shoved me back against the bed before turning away. The door slammed hard enough to rattle the window glass.

The house fell silent again.

I sat there for a long time, my cheek throbbing and my hands trembling in my lap. Outside, snow continued to fall in quiet spirals, drifting through the darkness like ash.

Eventually I crawled to the window and wrapped my arms around my knees.

I whispered verses into the darkness the way she had taught me.

But the words felt hollow.

Empty.

And deep inside my chest, beneath the fear and the shame, something warm still flickered.

Not gone.

Not punished.

Waiting.

Chapter Three

Under the Big Top

Ink and Fire

By morning, the fog had thinned, drifting slowly away from the field like a curtain being drawn back after a long performance.

But the feeling inside my chest hadn't faded.

If anything, it had grown stronger.

It pulsed beneath my ribs like a second heartbeat, steady and insistent, growing louder the deeper I wandered into the circus encampment.

The tents were pitched in crooked rows across the damp grass, their red and black canvas faded with age. Some leaned slightly to one side as though they had settled too long into the earth beneath them.

Yet despite their worn appearance, the air around them felt alive.

Canvas shifted softly in the breeze. Lanterns swayed from ropes tied between iron stakes. Everywhere I looked there was movement— small signs of life tucked between shadows.

The circus breathed.

People moved between the tents now.

Or… something close enough to people that my mind struggled to tell the difference.

A tall man passed me carrying a stack of wooden crates, the skin along his jaw stretched strangely tight across his bones. When he turned his head, I caught a glimpse of scales along the side of his neck, shimmering faintly like fish skin beneath the morning light.

A woman walked beside him with mirrored lenses where her eyes should have been. They reflected the entire encampment back at me in fractured pieces.

Others moved through the space just as quietly.

A performer whose arms bent at angles that made my stomach tighten.

A boy whose shadow lagged half a second behind his steps.

None of them stared.

Not openly.

But I could feel their awareness sliding across my skin every time I passed.

They knew I was there.

They simply didn't seem surprised by it.

No one asked who I was.

No one asked why I had arrived.

It was as if the circus had known I was coming and had already decided I belonged.

I followed the sound of voices toward the largest tent near the center of the grounds. Strands of wooden beads hung across the entrance like a curtain, clacking softly when I pushed through them.

Inside, the space opened into something enormous.

The interior stretched upward like a cathedral made of canvas and rusted iron. Sunlight slipped through the seams high above, spilling down in pale golden beams that caught the drifting dust in the air.

The circus ring sat in the center of it all.

And that's where I saw her.

Sabine.

She stood barefoot on the packed dirt, one hip angled lazily as if the entire space belonged to her. A torch burned in her hand, its flame curling upward like a living thing reaching toward the ceiling.

Her hair fell down her back in thick black waves, catching small sparks of light as she moved. Her skin gleamed bronze beneath the lantern glow, every muscle along her arms and shoulders defined with effortless strength.

There was something almost predatory about the way she held herself.

Not tense.

Not cautious.

Simply aware of her own power.

She lifted the torch slowly.

The flame brightened as it rose.

For a moment she studied it, the fire reflected in her dark eyes.

Then she brought it to her lips.

My breath caught in my throat.

Sabine inhaled deeply, drawing the flame into her mouth in one smooth motion.

The fire vanished.

The torch went dark.

A ripple of murmured applause drifted from somewhere deeper inside the tent.

Sabine tilted her head back slightly and exhaled.

Smoke slipped from her lips in a thin, curling stream, drifting upward toward the rafters like a prayer that had lost its way.

She turned then.

And her eyes met mine.

Amber.

Ancient.

There was something in them that made my stomach twist in a way I didn't understand.

I looked away too quickly.

My pulse had begun to race.

That was when I felt someone step close behind me.

"Pretty, isn't she?"

The voice brushed across my ear like velvet dragged slowly over skin.

I turned.

Lilith stood beside me.

She was taller than I expected, her height giving her an effortless presence that filled the space around her. Her skin was pale enough to catch the faintest glow of the lanterns overhead, almost luminous in the dim light.

Black ink curled across every visible inch of her.

Tattoos climbed her arms in winding patterns—vines and serpents twisting together with shapes that resembled stars or wings. Some symbols I recognized from old religious texts. Others looked older than anything I had ever seen.

Her eyes were violet.

Not the soft purple of flowers.

Something darker.

Something magical.

They studied me openly, without apology.

My gaze drifted to the tattoo just beneath her collarbone.

A small flame.

It burned beneath the outline of black wings.

"She bites, you know," Lilith said casually, her lips curving slightly.

She leaned closer as she spoke, her breath warm near my ear.

"But only if you ask nicely."

Heat rushed into my face before I could stop it.

I wasn't sure which part of her comment unsettled me more—the words themselves or the quiet amusement in her voice.

She noticed.

Of course she noticed.

Lilith tilted her head slightly, studying my reaction with the patient curiosity of a cat deciding whether its prey was worth chasing.

"You're new," she said.

I nodded.

My voice had disappeared somewhere between my lungs and my mouth.

She stepped closer.

The faint scent of smoke clung to her skin.

"You smell like shame," she murmured thoughtfully.

Her fingers lifted slowly, brushing along my jaw.

The touch was light.

Almost gentle.

But the warmth of it spread through my entire body in a way that made my pulse stutter.

"And smoke," she added softly.

Her eyes flicked briefly toward the circus ring where Sabine still stood holding the torch.

"Don't worry."

Her thumb traced the line of my chin before she pulled her hand away.

"It washes off."

A laugh drifted across the tent.

Low.

Amused.

Sabine.

Lilith's lips curved into a small smile, the color of crushed berries staining them dark.

"Come find me when you're ready to burn," she whispered.

And then she stepped away.

One moment she was beside me.

The next she had vanished into the shadows between the hanging curtains and support poles, slipping through the tent like smoke through open fingers.

I stood alone near the entrance.

Dust drifted lazily through the sunlight overhead.

My heart hammered against my ribs so hard it almost hurt.

My mouth had gone dry.

I shouldn't have reacted like that.

Not to a stranger.

Not to a woman.

Not to two of them.

But the feeling lingered long after they were gone.

Sharp.

Unsettling.

And somewhere beneath the confusion, another truth stirred quietly inside my chest.

I wanted to feel it again.

Chapter Four

Before the Circus

Church and Control

The bells of St. Augustine's rang across the town like a warning.

Their heavy toll rolled through the cold morning air, echoing off stone buildings and narrow streets until the sound seemed impossible to escape. Each strike vibrated through the floorboards beneath my feet as I stood inside the church with my hands folded tightly together.

The scent of incense hung thick in the air, sweet and suffocating. It coated the back of my throat and filled my lungs until breathing felt like swallowing smoke.

My mother knelt beside me in the pew, her posture rigid and perfectly straight. The rosary wound tightly through her fingers, each bead sliding beneath her thumb with quiet precision.

Click.
Whisper.
Click.
Whisper.

Each prayer that left her lips sounded less like devotion and more like a command.

"Eyes down," she murmured without turning her head.

Her voice was soft enough that no one else would hear it, but sharp enough to cut straight through me.

I lowered my gaze immediately.

My heart pounded against my ribs.

I had looked.

Only for a second.

But she had seen.

Three rows ahead sat a girl I had never noticed before. Her hair shone pale gold beneath the colored light streaming through the stained glass windows, the ribbon at the base of her neck tied in a careful bow. When she had stepped into the pew earlier, she turned slightly.

Our eyes met.

Just for a moment.

But something inside my chest had unraveled the instant it happened.

Warm.

Strange.

Dangerous.

Her gaze had slipped away quickly, returning to the altar as though nothing had happened.

But the feeling remained.

A quiet spark beneath my ribs.

I didn't know what it meant.

I only knew it felt wrong.

My mother's hand closed around my wrist.

Hard.

Her nails dug into my skin until I felt the sharp sting of them breaking the surface. She didn't say a word. She didn't need to.

By the time Mass ended, the marks would be there—small crescents pressed into my flesh like tiny reminders of my failure.

When the final hymn ended, the congregation began to rise. Wooden pews creaked and coats rustled as people gathered their belongings.

Before I could stand fully, my mother seized my wrist again.

"Come."

The word wasn't loud.

But it carried the weight of an order.

She dragged me down the narrow aisle toward the side chapel, my shoes sliding against the cold stone floor as I struggled to keep pace. The chapel door swung open with a hollow creak.

Inside, the air was darker.

Quieter.

The confessional stood against the far wall like a wooden coffin waiting patiently for its occupant.

"You will confess," she said.

I hesitated.

Her hand shoved firmly between my shoulders.

I stumbled forward into the narrow booth, the door closing behind me with a soft but final click. The small sliding panel in the lattice opened.

"Yes, my child?"

The priest's voice drifted through the screen.

Low.

Measured.

Patient in the way men often sounded when they believed they already understood your soul better than you did.

I swallowed hard. My hands twisted together in my lap.

"What sins burden your soul?" he asked.

My mouth opened.

Nothing came out.

The silence stretched until it felt unbearable.

Finally, I forced the words through the tightness in my throat.

"I… had a thought."

"Speak it."

My eyes fixed on the dim wooden floor.

"I looked at a girl."

The quiet that followed felt heavier than any punishment.

"I don't know why," I continued quickly. "But I… I felt something."

My fingers tightened against each other.

"I think it was wrong."

Another pause.

Then the priest spoke again.

"Impure thoughts are the gateway to damnation," he said calmly. "Confession is the first step toward salvation, but only if your heart truly desires to be cleansed."

My chest tightened.

"The Lord does not forgive what you still long for," he continued. "You must root it out entirely."

A dull ache formed in my stomach.

"These thoughts are not yours. They are whispers from the Devil himself. He enters through temptation. Through weakness."

My teeth pressed against the inside of my cheek until I tasted blood.

"Do not mistake curiosity for innocence," the priest added. "Corruption begins in the smallest moments."

The panel slid shut.

My confession was finished.

When I stepped out of the booth, my mother was already waiting. She studied my face carefully, her expression unreadable.

Then she nodded once toward the iron gate leading to the back of the church.

No words.

None were necessary.

We walked home in silence.

The wind cut across the street, biting at my cheeks and ears. But the cold outside was nothing compared to the burning shame spreading beneath my skin.

By the time we reached the house, my stomach had twisted itself into tight knots.

Mother opened the door and stepped inside.

"Upstairs," she said.

I obeyed.

The bedroom felt colder than the church.

"Remove your dress," she said.

I did.

"Fold it neatly."

I placed it on the chair beside the bed.

She carried the steel washbasin into the room and set it heavily on the floor. The metal rang softly against the wood as it settled. Without a word, she filled it with water from the well.

Then she stepped outside.

When she returned, she carried a block of ice wrapped in cloth.

She struck it once with the fireplace poker.

The ice cracked with a sharp snap.

Fragments tumbled into the basin, floating across the water like broken glass.

"You want to feel things you shouldn't," she said flatly.

The cold in her voice frightened me more than her shouting ever had.

"Let's remind you what feeling truly is."

"Please," I whispered.

"God sees everything," she said. "And I will not allow filth beneath my roof."

Her hand gripped the back of my neck.

She forced me down beside the basin.

"You will repent."

"Mother—"

The water swallowed my cry.

My head plunged beneath the surface as ice pressed against my cheeks and scalp. The shock stole the air from my lungs instantly. I thrashed, but her grip held firm.

When she pulled me back up, I gasped for breath.

"What does it say?" she demanded.

My teeth chattered violently.

"Leviticus," she snapped.

"'Thou shalt not lie with mankind—'"

"Louder."

"'Thou shalt not lie with mankind as with womankind; it is abomination!'"

The water closed over my head again.

This time I inhaled some of it before she lifted me back out.

"You will be pure," she said coldly. "You will not burn in Hell for unnatural desires."

Tears streamed down my face, though I could barely feel them anymore.

I wasn't sure whether I was crying from the cold or from the shame.

Or from the quiet truth that refused to disappear.

I had liked the way the girl looked at me.

That small warmth from the church still flickered somewhere inside me, stubborn and alive despite everything.

"God made woman to serve man," my mother continued, pacing slowly around me. "To be obedient. To be silent. To be clean."

My body trembled violently beside the basin.

When I finally collapsed onto the floor, she stood over me and crossed herself.

"Lord," she prayed aloud, "purge this child of sin. Remove what Satan has planted inside her soul."

Her shadow stretched across the floor.

"Make her pure in Your eyes."

I don't remember when sleep finally took me.

Only the numbness spreading slowly through my limbs.

And a single, dangerous thought forming quietly beneath the cold.

If this was the God she served…

I wasn't sure I wanted Him at all.

Chapter Five

Under the Big Top

The Midnight Show

By the time the bells in the distance struck midnight, the circus had transformed. The quiet encampment I had wandered through earlier in the day had vanished beneath a new kind of energy. Lanterns burned along every path, casting golden halos across the damp grass while music drifted between the tents—violins weaving through the steady thrum of drums, laughter rising and falling like waves against canvas walls. And all of it seemed to lead toward the largest tent at the center of the grounds.

The Big Top.

I hesitated at the entrance, staring up at the towering canvas. The fabric rippled softly in the wind, the red and black stripes twisting together like something alive. Lanterns burned along the ropes anchoring it to the earth, their flames flickering in restless patterns that made the shadows dance across the ground.

People poured inside. Some looked like ordinary travelers bundled against the cold night air, but others did not. A tall man ducked beneath the entrance flap, his shoulders so wide they nearly brushed both sides of the opening. As he turned his head, lantern light passed straight through his thin skin, his veins glowed faintly like threads of molten glass. A woman followed behind him, antlers rising from her dark curls, the bone tips wrapped in thin strands of silver chain that chimed softly whenever she moved. No one seemed frightened. No one stared. No one even seemed surprised. The circus accepted them all, and somehow… it had accepted me.

I slipped inside.

The air beneath the tent shimmered with warmth. Hundreds of lanterns hung from iron rings overhead, their light softened by drifting smoke and dust. Velvet benches circled the ring in wide rows already filling with murmuring spectators. Perfume lingered in the air alongside sweat and something sharper I couldn't quite identify—like the metallic scent that followed a lightning strike. I slid quietly onto a bench near the back and folded my hands in my lap, trying to steady the restless pulse beating inside my chest.

The tent filled quickly. Boots thudded against the packed dirt floor while conversations overlapped in low murmurs. Someone nearby uncorked a bottle and the sharp scent of liquor drifted through the air. Anticipation seemed to hum in the canvas above our heads.

Then, slowly, the lanterns began to dim.

One by one.

Until the tent sank into darkness.

The crowd quieted, and for a moment there was nothing but silence. Then the drum began. A single deep beat rolled through the darkness, low and heavy, slow and steady. It sounded almost like a heartbeat buried beneath the earth. Another beat followed. Then another. The rhythm spread through the tent until it vibrated through the wooden benches beneath us, thrumming up through the soles of my boots.

A golden light unfurled across the center ring.

Madame Thorne stepped into it.

The entire tent seemed to lean forward. Her gown shimmered black beneath the lantern glow, the fabric catching the light in shifting ripples like oil on water. Dark kohl framed her eyes, stretching their shape into something dramatic and predatory. She looked less like a ringmaster and more like a queen surveying her kingdom. Her gaze drifted slowly across the audience—calculating, knowing—and when she spoke, her voice carried effortlessly through the tent.

"Welcome."

The word curled through the air like smoke.

"Welcome," she continued softly, "to the Unholy and Uncaged."

She began to pace slowly around the ring, her cane tapping lightly against the dirt floor. "To those the world feared. Tap. To those they chained. Tap. To those they buried. Tap. To those they burned." Her lips curved into a slow smile as the final words settled over the audience. "And yet… here you stand."

The smile deepened.

"Welcome to the beautiful damned."

Her cane struck the dirt with a sharp crack, and light burst outward across the ring like a living current. The show began.

The first performer stepped into the glow like a ghost. She looked fragile enough to shatter, her skin nearly white beneath the lantern light with thin blue veins visible along her wrists and throat. Long strings stretched from her arms toward the rafters high above, but there was no puppeteer. The drumbeat quickened slightly as she lifted one foot. Her body jerked sharply, then she spun.

The movement was perfect.

Precise.

Impossible.

Her limbs twisted through graceful arcs, each motion pulled by invisible hands. Her joints bent at unnatural angles as she danced, arching backward so far her hair brushed the dirt. Her eyes were cloudy, milky, empty. The strings snapped suddenly and her body jerked upward into a violent spin before dropping into a delicate pirouette. The audience gasped.

Someone whispered behind me.

"She died once."

A chill crept along my spine as the girl continued dancing, her expression never changing.

The lights shifted again, darkening the edges of the ring. A tall man stepped forward, shirtless, his body marked with dozens of scars— thin white lines crisscrossing his chest and shoulders like lightning etched into flesh. His eyes were completely black. No white. No reflection. Just darkness. A whip hung loosely from his hand.

At first I thought the creatures that followed him were animals.

Then one lifted its head.

They had once been human. I could still see it in their faces, though something had changed them. One dragged itself forward with a long scaled tail coiling behind it like a serpent's body. Another's neck fluttered with thin gills that opened and closed with every breath. A third looked almost human until she smiled, rows of sharp teeth glinting in the lantern light.

The Beast Tamer cracked the whip once.

The sound echoed through the tent like thunder.

The creatures froze instantly—not in fear, but in anticipation. Their eyes gleamed in the lantern light: green, gold, silver, hungry. The audience applauded wildly.

I pressed my hand against my chest.

I should have been horrified.

Instead… I couldn't stop watching.

The lantern glow shifted again, this time deepening into crimson. Lilith stepped into the ring, and a hush fell across the tent. She wore a sheer black corset and loose bloomers tied at her hips while lantern light shimmered across her pale skin, illuminating the intricate tattoos covering nearly every inch of her body. Dragons curled along her ribs, vines wrapped around her arms, eyes stared from her shoulders.

At first they looked like ordinary tattoos.

Then one blinked.

A murmur rippled through the crowd as Lilith began to move. Her dance was slow and deliberate, every motion controlled. As she turned, the ink shifted across her skin like living creatures. A dragon slithered along her spine, its wings unfurling as she arched backward. A rose along her thigh bloomed open in deep crimson petals while a serpent curled around her waist and slid slowly downward.

Gasps filled the tent.

Her violet eyes lifted.

They found mine instantly.

A slow smile touched her lips.

I looked away quickly, but the heat rising in my face told me she had already seen everything.

Then Sabine stepped into the ring.

The entire tent seemed to inhale.

She moved barefoot across the dirt with flames dancing easily between her palms as though they were nothing more dangerous than water. Her hair spilled down her back in thick dark waves while the dress she wore clung to her body like a second skin. Freckles scattered across her shoulders, her skin glowing in the firelight.

She lifted her hands.

The flames followed.

They spiraled up her arms like golden ribbons before leaping outward into the air. She spun once, twice, the fire trailing behind her in blazing circles as the crowd roared in approval.

But Sabine wasn't watching them.

Her gaze drifted slowly through the tent.

Until it found me.

The moment our eyes met, something inside my chest ignited. The warmth beneath my skin surged suddenly and my fingers began to tingle. I looked down.

Light pulsed faintly beneath the skin of my palms.

Golden.

Like embers buried deep in ash.

My pulse raced as the glow spread slowly along the veins of my wrists. Someone beside me gasped. Panic shot through me and I shoved my hands beneath my thighs, but the heat didn't stop.

In the center ring Sabine spun once more and fire erupted around her in a brilliant arc. Her body arched backward, arms outstretched as flames curled from her mouth like a dragon's breath. The audience exploded into applause.

But the world around me had begun to tilt.

The warmth vanished from my hands as suddenly as it had appeared. Lantern lights blurred together while the tent seemed to sway around me.

Sabine's face appeared closer now.

Her expression unreadable.

Concerned.

Or curious.

I tried to stand.

The tent lurched sideways.

My knees buckled.

And darkness rushed up to meet me.

Chapter Six

Before the Circus

Vanishing Father

I always knew he was leaving before he said a word.

My father packed quietly, as if keeping the house silent might somehow soften the act of leaving. He folded his shirts with slow, deliberate movements, his calloused hands smoothing the fabric as though it might remember him when he was gone. When he finished, he slipped his leather Bible into his satchel, tucking it carefully beside the few other belongings he carried with him.

Sometimes he knelt beside the hearth in his old work boots, pretending to stir the dying coals.

Pretending he wasn't about to walk out the door again.

The firelight flickered across his face while he worked, carving tired shadows beneath his eyes. When he finally looked at me, there was always something there I didn't know how to name. Weariness. Guilt. Or perhaps something closer to shame.

"I'll be back in a few weeks," he would say.

He never said goodbye.

My father worked the rails. That was the explanation he gave anyone who asked. He repaired telegraph lines, helped with rail maintenance crews, traveled wherever the work carried him. At least, that was what he said.

But sometimes he returned home with bruised knuckles and eyes that seemed to look through me rather than at me, and I suspected the work was not always what he claimed.

He was gone for weeks at a time.

Sometimes months.

Always chasing money.

Or maybe chasing something quieter—something that existed far away from our house.

He called it God's provision. Said that a man who worked hard for his family was doing holy work.

But nothing about his absence ever felt holy to me.

And when he was home, I still didn't feel protected.

"She's a good girl when you're here," my mother used to tell him.

He always believed her.

And I always paid for it once he left.

The morning he departed that winter, I was kneeling on the kitchen floor scrubbing soot from beneath the wood stove. The rag bucket sat beside me, the water inside already dark with ash. My hands stung from the cold and the lye soap, the skin along my knuckles cracked and sore.

I reached for the rag again.

My elbow caught the bucket.

The water tipped.

It spilled across the floor in a black, spreading puddle.

Panic rushed through me instantly. I dropped to my hands and knees, trying to gather the water back with the edge of my skirts, but she was already standing behind me.

My mother's shadow stretched across the floor before her voice came.

"You think this is amusing?"

I froze.

Her silhouette filled the doorway.

"You think ruining this home pleases God?"

"No, ma'am," I said quickly, my voice trembling.

"You mock His blessings with your filth," she continued, her tone sharpening with each word. "You mock me."

She grabbed the worn family Bible from the table and shoved it into my lap.

"Recite," she ordered. "Proverbs thirty-one. Now."

The pages shook slightly as I opened them.

"She riseth also while it is yet night," I began quietly, "and giveth meat to her household…"

"Louder."

My throat tightened as I continued. I stumbled on the next verse, my voice catching as I spoke the wrong word.

The slap came before I could correct myself.

My head snapped to the side as heat bloomed across my cheek.

"Blasphemer," she hissed. "You twist His word."

"I'm sorry," I whispered.

The apology felt hollow even as I said it.

I wasn't sorry for the mistake.

I was sorry that I still didn't know how to fight back.

That night the house filled with the smell of candle smoke. My mother knelt beside her bed, whispering prayers under her breath with the same rigid intensity she brought to everything else. The words blended together until they sounded less like devotion and more like a ritual she performed out of habit.

While she prayed, I crept quietly up the narrow staircase to the attic.

A loose board beneath the eaves lifted easily under my fingers.

Inside the hollow space beneath it lay my secret.

A worn composition book.

And a pencil shaved nearly down to nothing.

I sat cross-legged on the floor and began to write.

I wrote about girls with wings who could fly beyond the reach of church bells and locked doors. I wrote about storms I could summon with a scream. I wrote about kissing someone in a field of ash where no one watched and nothing burned.

Sometimes the words came so quickly I could barely keep up with them. Other nights I wrote letters to my father.

Letters I never sent.

When I turned thirteen, I tried telling him the truth.

He stood beside the gate that morning, tightening the loose latch with a small wrench while I hovered nearby, unsure how to begin. Finally the words spilled out before I could lose my nerve.

"She makes me kneel on rice," I said. "She says I'm cursed. She says I'm like her. I don't even know who that is."

My father looked at me slowly.

For a moment he seemed confused, as though my voice had reached him from somewhere far away.

"Your mother's strict," he said carefully. "But she's a godly woman."

"I'm not lying."

He sighed and rubbed a hand down his face.

"You've always had a vivid imagination, Evie," he said. "But you need to be careful about what you say."

"She hits me," I whispered.

"She hurts me."

He looked tired.

Not angry.

Not shocked.

Just tired.

"She prays for you every night," he said quietly. "Sometimes love looks like correction."

My throat burned.

"You're getting older," he added. "Maybe you need a little more discipline."

Coming from him those words struck harder than any slap from my mother ever did.

He leaned down and kissed the top of my head as though that gesture alone might repair everything.

Then he turned and walked back toward the house.

I didn't run that year.

I stayed.

I stayed through the long winter that frosted the windows from the inside. I stayed through the spring when my mother called my growing body a temptation and forced me to wear heavy skirts even in the heat. I stayed through the summer when she caught me staring too long at the butcher's daughter and made me kneel in a basin of dried beans until the skin on my knees blistered.

By then I was almost seventeen.

And somewhere along the way…

I stopped praying.

Chapter Seven

Under the Big Top

Initiation

The circus never truly slept.

Even in the quiet hours between dusk and dawn, life moved through the encampment like a restless tide. Music drifted between the tents in slow wandering melodies—violins tuning somewhere in the fog, the low pulse of a drum carried on the wind like a distant heartbeat. Lanterns burned low along the winding paths, their flames trembling in the mist while the scent of firewood lingered in the air, mingling with perfume and damp earth.

Somewhere in the distance someone laughed.

Elsewhere, someone cried.

The circus breathed through it all.

Two nights had passed since I collapsed during the Midnight Show, yet the memory still clung to me in fragments. Sabine's fire swirling through the air. The heat rising beneath my skin. The sudden glow of my hands like embers breaking through ash.

No one spoke of it openly.

When I asked, they told me I had fainted from excitement. From the warmth of the flames. From the overwhelming spectacle of the performance. Too much wonder, they said.

But I knew better.

I had never felt more awake than I had in that moment—when Sabine danced with the fire and something buried deep inside my chest answered her.

Now I sat alone on the wooden steps outside a small tent stitched with silver stars. The canvas shimmered faintly in the lantern light, the embroidery catching the glow like distant constellations. Fog drifted slowly across the ground, curling around the base of the central ring, and above me the sky was thick with clouds that hid the stars completely.

Still, I could feel them.

A quiet pressure beyond the veil.

Something ancient humming just out of sight.

Footsteps approached behind me.

I turned.

Madame Thorne emerged from the mist as though the darkness itself had shaped her. Her long robes trailed across the ground, the fabric whispering softly with each step. When her eyes met mine, they carried the same unsettling calm they always had—old, patient, and kind in a way that felt dangerous.

"You're quieter than usual," she said.

Her voice moved through the air like smoke.

I hesitated before answering. "Was it real?" I asked finally. "What happened to my hands?"

She studied me for a long moment.

Then she nodded once.

"More real," she said softly, "than anything you've ever been allowed to believe."

A chill passed through me and my fingers curled slightly against my palms.

She extended her hand.

"Come," she said. "It's time."

She led me through the winding paths of the encampment. Lantern light flickered along the canvas walls of the tents as we passed. Shadows moved behind some of them—performers adjusting costumes, voices murmuring in languages I didn't recognize. The circus felt different at night. Less like a show and more like a living organism breathing quietly in the dark.

From one open tent drifted the scent of honey and smoke. Inside, a woman sat braiding sparks into a length of golden thread. No one paid her any attention.

We stopped just beyond the fire pit at the center of the grounds.

A small group waited there.

Sabine leaned against one of the wooden support posts, one bare foot braced behind her against the timber. Small flames danced lazily along her fingertips, flaring and fading like tiny living creatures. When she saw me, she straightened slightly.

Our eyes met.

Something inside my chest tightened instantly, as if a thread had been pulled between us.

Sabine smiled.

Slow.

Dangerous.

Heat rushed into my face before I could stop it.

"Emotion is magic," Madame Thorne said quietly. Her voice carried easily through the cool night air. "It has always been so. The world you came from simply feared it."

She turned toward me.

"There, emotion was punished. Controlled. Silenced."

Her eyes softened slightly.

"Here, we honor it."

I swallowed.

"Feed it," she added.

Confusion twisted in my chest. "What am I?" I asked.

Madame Thorne regarded me thoughtfully before answering.

"You," she said slowly, "are a vessel."

The word lingered in the air.

"A spark waiting for flame. A match waiting to be struck."

She stepped aside.

Sabine moved toward me.

Each step she took sent a strange shiver through my body. I could smell smoke on her skin now—warm and sweet, touched with cinnamon and something wild I couldn't quite place.

When she reached me, her fingers brushed lightly against my wrist.

The contact was barely there.

But it was enough.

The warmth returned instantly.

It began low in my stomach and spread outward in slow curling waves, like smoke rising through my ribs. My breath caught as the sensation deepened, building into something fierce and bright.

It wasn't pain.

But it wasn't calm either.

It was sharper than either of those things.

Wanting.

Sabine's expression shifted slightly as she felt it too.

"You're burning," she murmured.

"I—what?"

I glanced down.

Golden light shimmered beneath the skin of my palms. Tiny flames flickered along my fingertips like living embers.

Sabine didn't pull away.

Instead, she stepped closer.

"You feel it," she said softly. "The way your body answers when it's seen."

My heart hammered violently against my ribs.

"I don't understand," I whispered.

"You don't have to," she replied gently. "Just let it happen."

She placed her palm against mine.

The moment our hands touched, the fire surged.

Flames burst along my arms in thin glowing ribbons, racing across my skin like threads of living light. I gasped and staggered backward as heat poured through my body, but the fire did not burn.

It danced.

Alive.

Emotion crashed through me all at once—fear, shame, freedom, desire. Every feeling I had ever buried rose to the surface together, twisting into something powerful and wild.

Madame Thorne stepped forward, her eyes bright with recognition.

"She's ready," she said quietly.

Sabine nodded slowly.

I looked between them, my breath unsteady. "What's happening to me?"

"You're becoming," Madame Thorne replied.

Her voice softened.

"Your body remembers what your mind was taught to forget."

She gestured toward the flames still dancing faintly along my arms.

"Emotion is not weakness," she said. "It is power."

"And yours," she added, "is waking."

Sabine's thumb brushed lightly across my knuckles.

"You feel everything," she said.

"That's your gift."

She held my gaze.

"And your danger."

"I don't know how to control it," I admitted.

"You will," she said quietly. "We'll help you."

Later that night they gave me a tent of my own.

The interior was unlike anything I had ever seen. Silk curtains draped the walls in deep shades of plum and midnight blue, while mirrors hung between the folds of fabric, catching lantern light and scattering it across the space in soft glowing fragments.

A small shelf held books bound in cracked leather.

Spells.

Stories.

Things I had never been allowed to read.

A costume waited for me on the bed.

The fabric was deep plum threaded with silver embroidery that curled like drifting smoke across the bodice. Beside it rested a delicate mask shaped like the wings of a moth.

Madame Thorne paused at the entrance before leaving.

"The Girl in Smoke," she said quietly.

The title hung in the air.

"Born of fire. Rising from shame."

Her gaze softened slightly.

"You are not what they tried to make you."

Then she disappeared into the night.

I stood alone in the quiet tent.

The robe hung loosely around my shoulders as I stared down at my hands. The warmth from Sabine's touch still lingered in my skin.

Outside, the circus hummed with distant music and laughter.

Life.

Inside the tent, the faint glow beneath my palms slowly brightened.

The feeling didn't fill me with guilt.

It filled me with something else entirely.

Something sharp.

Something thrilling.

Something dangerous.

And somewhere deep inside my chest, I realized I liked it.

Chapter Eight

Under the Big Top

The Morning After

Morning in the circus did not arrive the way it had in the town I left behind. There were no church bells calling the day into order, no rigid routine waiting to claim the hours before they had even begun. Instead, the world woke slowly. Light filtered through the canvas of my tent in pale golden patches that shifted gently as the wind moved outside. Somewhere beyond the fabric walls I heard the distant creak of wagon wheels, the murmur of voices, and the faint clang of metal striking metal.

The circus was waking.

I lay still for a long moment, staring up at the embroidered ceiling where silver-threaded constellations shimmered faintly in the morning light. For the first time in as long as I could remember, my chest did not feel tight with dread. No footsteps in the hall. No voice calling my name like a warning. Just quiet.

I pushed myself upright slowly. The robe they had given me the night before slipped from my shoulders in a soft cascade of plum-colored fabric, the silver embroidery curling along the sleeves like drifting smoke. When I rested my hands in my lap, the faint warmth beneath my skin was still there. It was not wild like it had been during the initiation. Not dangerous. Just present, like an ember waiting beneath ash.

Outside the tent, laughter drifted through the morning air.

Curiosity pulled me to my feet.

When I stepped outside, the world unfolded around me in a quiet spectacle. Morning mist still clung low to the ground, curling lazily between the tents like pale ghosts reluctant to leave. Lanterns burned along the paths, their flames dimming in the growing daylight while performers moved through the encampment in loose clusters. The circus looked different in the morning. Less like a performance. More like a village.

Someone had set up a long wooden table near the fire pit, covered with mismatched cups and steaming kettles. A man with bronze feathers instead of hair sat sharpening knives while a girl nearby practiced balancing on a thin wire stretched between two posts. No one seemed surprised to see me. A few heads turned in quiet acknowledgment. Someone lifted a hand in greeting.

I nodded awkwardly and continued down the path.

The smell of fresh bread drifted through the air, warm and comforting enough to make my stomach tighten with sudden hunger. I followed the scent to a small wagon where a woman stood beside a cast iron stove, flipping something golden in a skillet.

She glanced up when she saw me.

"You must be the new one," she said cheerfully.

I blinked. "Is it that obvious?"

She laughed and wrapped a piece of warm bread in cloth before pressing it into my hands. "Eat," she said. "You'll need it."

The bread was still hot enough that butter melted instantly across the surface. The first bite nearly made my eyes close.

"Better than church wafers, isn't it?" she added with a wink before turning back to her cooking.

I wandered further into the encampment as the sun slowly climbed higher. Everywhere I looked there were small wonders that seemed perfectly ordinary to everyone except me. A boy sitting cross-legged beside a wagon coaxed tiny glowing orbs from the air between his fingers, letting them drift upward like floating fireflies. A woman brushed her long silver hair while a flock of birds perched calmly along her shoulders. Two acrobats practiced flips near the ring, their movements so fluid it barely looked like gravity touched them at all.

No one stared.

No one questioned why I was there.

They simply accepted me.

The realization settled quietly in my chest.

I belonged here.

Or at least… I was allowed to try.

"Careful."

The voice came from behind me.

Warm. Amused.

I turned and found Sabine standing a few steps away, watching me with that same crooked smile she had worn the night before. In the daylight she looked different. Her dark hair was pulled loosely over one shoulder, and the freckles scattered across her nose and cheeks were more visible now. She wore a sleeveless black shirt and loose trousers, her bare feet dusted with pale dirt from the ground.

"You're wandering too close to the training ropes," she said.

I glanced down and realized I had nearly stepped into a stretch of wire where two performers were practicing knife throws.

I stepped back quickly. "Sorry."

Sabine laughed softly. "You'll learn."

Her gaze dropped to my hands.

"You feel it yet?"

"The fire?"

I hesitated. "A little."

Sabine stepped closer, not close enough to touch but close enough that I could smell the smoke on her skin.

"Show me."

My heart began beating faster. "I don't know how."

"You do," she said gently. "Stop trying to force it."

I looked down at my palms. They felt warm, but nothing happened.

Sabine reached out then, her fingers closing lightly around my wrist. The contact sent a sudden rush of heat up my arm.

"Relax," she murmured.

Her thumb brushed slowly across the inside of my wrist where my pulse fluttered.

"Your fire listens to your emotions."

My breath caught slightly. "That seems dangerous."

Sabine smiled. "It is."

She turned my hand slightly. "Now breathe."

I did.

The warmth beneath my skin stirred.

A tiny flame flickered to life between my fingers.

Small. Unsteady. But real.

My eyes widened.

Sabine's grin deepened.

"There you go."

The flame danced for a moment before fading back into warmth.

"I did that," I whispered.

"You did."

Her eyes lingered on mine for a moment longer than necessary before shifting past me.

"Careful, though."

I followed her gaze.

Across the clearing, Lilith leaned against one of the tent poles watching us. Her violet eyes glittered in the morning light while the black ink across her arms shifted subtly as she moved. When she realized I had noticed her, her lips curved into a faint smile.

Not warm.

Not cold.

Something far more complicated.

Sabine sighed softly. "She does that."

"Watches people?" I asked.

"Studies them," Sabine corrected. "For art."

I glanced back toward Lilith, but she was already slipping between the tents like smoke.

Sabine turned back to me. "You're going to fit in here."

"How can you tell?"

She nodded toward my hands.

"Because the circus already chose you."

The warmth beneath my skin flickered again—small, bright, alive.

And it didn't scare me.

Chapter Nine

Before the Circus

The Closet and the Fire

I knew something was wrong the moment I stepped into my room. The floorboard beneath the window—the one I had carefully pried loose months earlier to hide my journal—had been moved. Not simply shifted, but replaced with careful precision, the grain of the wood aligned so neatly it would have fooled anyone who didn't know exactly where to look. My stomach tightened as the realization settled over me.

Slowly, I lifted my gaze.

My mother sat at the small wooden table beside my bed as though she had been waiting for hours. My journal lay open in front of her, its worn pages spread flat beneath one pale hand while the other slowly threaded a rosary through her fingers. The candle beside her cast a weak golden light that stretched her shadow long across the floorboards.

She was reading.

"Her smile was like sunlight through stained glass," she said quietly, her eyes still fixed on the page. Her voice was calm—too calm. "Her hair golden, her skin porcelain. I wonder if she's soft beneath those pressed church clothes." She paused only long enough to turn another page before continuing. "I wonder what it would feel like to kiss her."

The air vanished from my lungs. My throat closed so suddenly I couldn't force a sound past it. I stood frozen near the doorway, every instinct in my body screaming for me to run, yet my feet refused to move.

At last she lifted her eyes.

There was no anger in them. No shouting. No wild fury. That quiet control frightened me far more.

"You dare write this filth?" she asked softly as she closed the journal with deliberate care. The rosary tightened around her fingers as she rose from the chair. "This… perversion. Under my roof. Under God's roof."

Her gaze moved slowly over my face as though she were examining something rotten.

"You filthy little whore."

"You are the Devil's work," she continued, her voice sharpening with each word. "I knew it the day you came into this world screaming like some feral beast."

"Mother—please—"

Her hand cracked across my face before I finished the sentence. Pain exploded through my cheek as my head snapped sideways, the taste of blood rising instantly in my mouth.

Before I could recover, she seized my arm.

Her grip was brutal.

She dragged me from the room without another word, pulling me down the narrow hallway as though I weighed nothing. My feet slipped against the floorboards as I struggled to keep my balance.

"Mother, please—you're hurting me—"

She didn't answer.

At the end of the corridor she stopped beside a small wooden door set low into the wall. It wasn't a closet in any normal sense of the word. It was a crawlspace carved into the bones of the house itself, barely large enough for someone to crouch inside.

The moment I saw it, my chest tightened.

"No," I whispered. "Please—don't put me in there."

She ignored me. Instead, she stepped past me and lifted the lid from a wooden crate sitting beside the wall. I hadn't noticed it before, but now the sour smell drifting from inside it made my stomach twist.

She tipped the crate forward.

Rats spilled out.

Dozens of them poured onto the floor in a gray writhing wave—fur, claws, and squealing bodies scattering across the boards. Their tiny feet scratched loudly against the wood as they scrambled in every direction.

My heart lurched violently.

"Mother—no—please—"

She drove them toward me with the toe of her shoe, herding them closer until they clustered against my skirts. Then she shoved me into the crawlspace and slammed the door shut behind me.

Darkness swallowed everything.

For a moment there was only the sound of my own breathing, sharp and panicked in the small space. The ceiling forced me to crouch while the damp stone walls pressed close on either side. Then something brushed against my ankle. I jerked violently as another small body darted across my calf, its claws scratching against my skin.

"No—no—"

My voice cracked as terror surged through me. The air inside smelled of mold and rot, thick enough that every breath felt heavy in my lungs.

Small bodies scurried up my legs, my wrist, my shoulder. Something cold brushed against the back of my neck.

Then teeth sank into my calf.

The pain was sudden and sharp, ripping a scream from my throat. I kicked blindly, trying to shake them off, but the movement only stirred them further. The rats erupted into frantic motion, their bodies scrambling over one another as they climbed across me in desperate bursts of claws and teeth.

Outside the door, my mother's voice rose calmly through the wood.

"The heart is deceitful above all things," she recited, "and desperately wicked. Who can know it?"

"MOTHER!" I screamed. "PLEASE!"

I clawed at the door, my fingernails scraping against the wood. Splinters dug into my skin as I pounded against the wood, panic surging through my chest, but the door didn't move.

"Flee from sexual immorality," she continued outside, her voice steady as a sermon. "Your body is a temple of the Holy Ghost."

"STOP!" I sobbed. "Please—please stop!"

Another rat bit into the side of my waist, its teeth sharp through the thin fabric of my dress. My breath came in ragged gasps as pain and terror twisted together inside my chest. I curled inward instinctively, trying to shield my face, but there was nowhere left to hide.

They were everywhere.

Their claws scratched against my arms and legs as they crawled over me, sniffing and biting. My skin burned in dozens of places as panic drained the strength from my limbs.

Outside, my mother continued quoting scripture as though my screams were simply part of the lesson she intended me to learn.

Then something changed.

At first it was only a faint sound.

A crackle.

It was different from the rats. Different from her voice. The air shifted suddenly, warming in a way that made the small space feel even tighter.

Smoke slipped through the cracks in the door.

The rats froze.

Then they scattered.

Outside, my mother's voice stopped.

Silence fell over the hallway.

"What have you done now?"

Her voice sounded different this time.

Uneasy.

The crackling grew louder.

The door trembled beneath my hands.

"WHAT DID YOU DO?"

The wood ripped open.

Light flooded the crawlspace.

Not sunlight.

Firelight.

The hallway behind her burned with bright orange flames, the fire licking along the walls and floorboards like hungry tongues. Smoke curled toward the ceiling as heat washed over the space.

She grabbed my arm and yanked me from the crawlspace as rats fled in every direction across the floor. The wallpaper along the hallway curled inward as the heat climbed higher, the corner of the table already beginning to burn.

"How?" she demanded, her voice shaking now. "How did you do this?"

"I didn't!" I coughed, choking on smoke. "I was locked in the closet!"

We both turned toward my bedroom.

The mattress burned.

The desk burned.

My journal lay in the center of my bed, untouched by the flames.

And then—

The fire vanished.

The flames collapsed inward like a breath being pulled back into a body. The smoke dissolved. The heat vanished from the air.

The walls stood untouched.

The curtain hung whole.

There wasn't even a scorch mark on the floor.

My mother stared at the hallway in stunned silence.

Her mouth opened slowly.

"You…" she whispered.

Her eyes turned toward me, wide with something I had never seen there before.

Fear.

"You did this."

Her voice dropped into a trembling whisper.

"You… thing."

I didn't answer.

I couldn't.

Because somewhere deep inside my chest—beneath the pain, the terror, and the shame—something still burned.

And it knew the truth.

The fire hadn't come to punish me.

It had come to set me free.

Chapter Ten

Under the Big Top

Sabine's Flame

"Feel it here," Madame Thorne instructed, pressing her hand gently just below my ribs. "That's where the magic begins. Not in your hands. Not in your thoughts. Your gut. Your feeling."

I stood in the center of the performance tent with my bare feet planted in the packed dirt. The ground was cool against my skin, but sweat clung to the back of my neck and slid slowly down my spine. The air inside the tent smelled of ash, lamp oil, and old canvas. Above us the massive fabric ceiling groaned softly as the wind shifted outside, the ropes creaking like something alive.

A flame flickered weakly in my palm.

It was small. Unsteady. Barely more than a trembling ember.

Nothing like Sabine's towering spirals of fire.

Sabine stood a few feet away, leaning lightly against one of the support poles. Her corseted waist curved beneath the lantern light, and her arms rested loosely across her chest as though she had been watching performers practice her entire life. Yet her eyes never drifted. They stayed on me with quiet patience.

Watching.

Always watching.

"Again," Madame Thorne said softly.

I swallowed and lifted my hand.

Focus.

Breathe.

I closed my eyes and tried to feel the warmth she had spoken about. Slowly, carefully, I searched for it inside myself. At first there was only tension in my chest and the faint tremble in my fingers. But then something deeper stirred beneath my ribs—heat blooming low and steady like coals buried in ash.

A pulse.

A promise.

The warmth began to rise.

Then something cold cut through it.

A memory.

It struck so suddenly that my breath caught in my throat.

Not claws.

Not darkness.

The church.

I stood in the center aisle with every head turned toward me. The wooden pews stretched in long rows on either side while the stained glass windows cast colored light across the floor like spilled blood.

My mother's hand clamped around the back of my neck.

"Tell them, "She whispered.

The pastor watched from the altar, his mouth pulled tight in disappointment. The elders stood beside him like judges waiting for a verdict.

"Tell them what you wrote."

My throat burned

"Tell them what you felt."

I shook my head, tears blurring the rows of faces staring back at me.

"Tell them," she said again, squeezing harder.

"I —"

The words tasted like poison.

"I looked at another girl."

The silence that followed was worse than shouting.

The memory slammed into me like a wave.

The flame in my palm sputtered.

Then vanished.

"Evelyn?"

Sabine's voice cut through the fog in my mind.

I opened my eyes just as the ground beneath my feet seemed to tilt. My chest tightened violently, as if iron bands had wrapped themselves around my ribs. Air refused to fill my lungs no matter how desperately I tried to inhale.

Not here.

Not now.

Before either of them could stop me, I turned and fled from the tent. The lantern light blurred as I stumbled past the fire barrels and pushed through the curtain at the entrance. I ran blindly until the open night air swallowed me, then collapsed behind a supply wagon where the earth was cold and damp.

My breaths came in quick, shallow gasps.

My heart pounded so hard it hurt.

I wrapped my arms around myself and rocked forward, trying to steady the trembling that had taken over my body. The dirt beneath my palms grounded me, but the panic still clawed its way through my chest.

The church, all their eyes and judgements on me.

You are not there. You are not there. You are not—

"Evelyn."

I flinched so hard my shoulders jerked.

Sabine crouched beside me, her crimson skirts spilling around her like dark petals. The lantern light from the tent caught in the waves of her hair, highlighting the copper undertones in the curls that had escaped from their pins. Her boots pressed into the earth as she leaned closer, studying me carefully.

"I'm fine," I managed between breaths.

Her brow lifted slightly.

"No, you're not."

She reached toward me, then paused before touching my hand. "May I?"

I nodded, still trembling.

Her fingers closed gently around mine, warm and steady. The simple contact grounded me more effectively than the cold earth beneath my knees ever had. Slowly she shifted closer and placed her other hand lightly against my chest, just above my racing heart.

The fire inside me stirred again.

But this time it didn't come with fear.

It came with heat.

My body recognized hers before my thoughts could catch up. The warmth beneath my ribs spread outward in slow, steady waves, replacing the sharp edges of panic with something deeper and more confusing.

Sabine watched my breathing carefully as it began to steady. "There you are. She murmured quietly. Her thumb brushed lightly across my knuckles. The warmth spread further. My heartbeat slowed. The world stopped spinning.

The flames inside me didn't retreat.

They changed.

They burned brighter.

For a long moment neither of us spoke. The night air moved softly through the circus grounds, carrying the distant sounds of laughter and music. But inside that small pocket of darkness beside the wagon, the rest of the world seemed very far away.

Sabine's gaze drifted down to my lips. Then back to my eyes.

I wasn't sure who leaned in first.

Perhaps it was both of us.

Our lips met softly, hesitant at first, as though neither of us fully trusted the moment. The contact sent a quiet spark through my chest that had nothing to do with magic. Her hand slid gently to the back of my neck, her fingers tangling lightly in my hair as she pulled me a little closer.

For a moment the world beyond that small space disappeared.

I could smell smoke on her skin.

Wine.

Something wild and warm that made my pulse quicken again.

My fingers curled instinctively against the laced edge of her corset as the fabric of her skirt brushed against my legs. The heat between us built slowly, quietly, until the fire inside my chest answered it.

And part of me didn't want to pull away.

But I did.

I broke the kiss and leaned back, my breath uneven and my heart racing for reasons that had nothing to do with fear.

"I'm sorry," I whispered. "I didn't mean—"

"Yes," Sabine said hoarsely, cutting me off.

Her eyes held mine.

"You did."

She stood then, brushing the dirt from her skirt before turning back toward the lantern light of the tent. Without another word she walked away, leaving me behind the wagon with my thoughts spinning and my pulse still hammering in my chest.

That night sleep refused to come.

I lay on the narrow cot inside my tent with the lantern dimmed low, staring up at the canvas ceiling as the circus murmured quietly outside. Laughter drifted through the night air along with the distant sound of music, but none of it reached the restless storm inside my chest.

Shame lingered there, yes.

It hovered at the edges of my thoughts like incense smoke after Mass.

But something else lived beside it now.

Something stronger.

I pressed one hand against my chest and the other against my thigh, remembering the warmth of Sabine's lips and the quiet hunger in her eyes. My skin tingled where she had touched me, little sparks of heat traveling slowly along my nerves.

When I whispered her name into the darkness, the memory returned so vividly that I could almost feel her hands again.

Not the kind of fire that destroys everything it touches.

The kind that makes you want to step closer to the flame.

Chapter Eleven

Under the Big Top

Freaks Like Me

The night before the circus opened its gates to the next city, the entire troupe gathered around the central firepit for dinner.

It was one of the few moments when the constant motion of the circus slowed. For once there were no ropes being tightened, no props being carried between tents, no performers rehearsing tricks beneath flickering lanterns. The air settled into a rare stillness as the fire crackled and the scent of roasted meat drifted through the cool night.

Someone had cooked root vegetables in a cast iron pot, heavy with spices that clung warmly to the air. Bowls were passed around the circle, along with thick slices of bread and dark wine poured from dusty bottles. Laughter moved easily through the group, softening even the harder faces that usually carried the strain of travel and performance.

Sabine sat beside me on a low wooden crate, her thigh pressed lightly against mine. The contact was casual enough that no one would question it, yet steady enough to ground me. Every time she shifted, the warmth of her body reminded me that I was not standing alone at the edge of the circle anymore.

Madame Thorne sat opposite us, pouring wine into chipped metal cups for the twins while listening quietly to their overlapping chatter. The Painted Man leaned back on his hands, smoke curling lazily from the bone pipe between his fingers. The scent of whatever he smoked was sharp and herbal, cutting through the heavier smell of food and fire.

Moth Girl fluttered around the circle like a restless spirit, her gauzy shawl catching the firelight as she moved. Even when she stood still the fabric shimmered faintly, giving the illusion of wings trembling in a breeze that wasn't there.

Lilith arrived last.

She always did.

She stepped into the firelight with the slow confidence of someone who understood exactly how the room shifted when she entered it. Her corset was laced tight around her waist, pushing the curve of her chest upward as the glow of the flames painted her skin in shades of copper and gold. A dark stain of wine colored her lips, and her hair had been pinned up with delicate silver combs that caught the light.

One loose curl had escaped, falling against the hollow of her collarbone.

She said nothing when she sat down.

She simply watched.

Moth Girl perched cross-legged in a way that no human joints should allow—tilted her head thoughtfully and asked, "What's the worst thing you've ever done?"

The question drifted around the circle like smoke.

At first there was laughter. A few groans. Someone muttered that it was a dangerous game to play among people like us.

But the answers came anyway.

One performer spoke in riddles about a priest who disappeared after a sermon. Another simply raised his wine cup and smiled without explaining anything at all. The twins whispered something to each other that ended in wicked laughter.

I stayed silent.

I didn't know what answer I would give even if someone asked me directly.

Then Sabine nudged Lilith's elbow with the side of her cup and nodded toward me. "Tell her about the tattoos."

Lilith raised one dark eyebrow.

"Curious, Evelyn?" she asked.

I hesitated before answering. "I thought they were just ink."

Her lips curved slightly.

"They're not."

Lilith rose from her seat with slow, deliberate grace. The firelight clung to her as she slipped her cloak from her shoulders and loosened the lacing of her corset just enough to reveal more of the intricate designs that covered her skin.

The ink was breathtaking.

At first glance it looked like a tapestry of elaborate tattoos—flowers, blades, animals, symbols I didn't recognize. But the longer I stared, the more something about them felt… wrong.

Alive.

"Each one appeared after something happened," Lilith explained, slipping the sleeve of her blouse down her shoulder so the ink along her arm caught the firelight. "I don't get to choose them."

The Painted Man exhaled a slow curl of smoke and nodded. "Magic ink," he said quietly. "It binds itself to the soul, not the skin."

I leaned forward despite myself.

A small dagger etched into her forearm shimmered faintly as the firelight moved. The blade caught the glow like polished glass. Near her hip, a rose bloomed in delicate detail, its petals shifting so subtly that I almost thought I imagined it.

Beneath her ribs sat something darker.

A faint handprint.

It looked bruised into her skin, unmoving and pale, as though a ghost had once pressed its palm there and never quite let go.

"They're stories," Lilith said calmly. "Punishments. Warnings. Promises."

"They move," I whispered.

She nodded once.

"When I lie. When I feel too much. When I dream."

Lilith turned slowly, letting the loosened corset slip lower so the firelight revealed her back. There, coiled between her shoulder blades, was a serpent drawn in deep black ink.

As we watched, the serpent blinked.

"This one appeared after I committed murder," she said.

The laughter around the fire vanished instantly.

The performers who had been joking moments before now watched her in silence.

"The man who hurt my sister," Lilith continued quietly. "I slit his throat while he slept."

The serpent on her back shifted slightly, its body tightening as if remembering the moment.

"It appeared the next morning," she said. "I tried to scrub it away. Soap. Steel wool. Even a blade."

Her fingers brushed the ink absently.

"It stayed."

"And the rose?" I asked.

Her eyes lifted and locked onto mine.

"The first girl I ever loved," Lilith said softly. "She died in a terrible accident. I believed for years that it was my fault."

The rose at her hip trembled.

"When I dream about her," she continued, "the petals move."

The fire popped loudly in the pit between us.

Someone shifted uncomfortably.

I couldn't tell whether the tight feeling in my chest was grief or relief.

"You're not the only strange one here, Evelyn," Lilith said gently.

She crossed the small distance between us and knelt in front of me, taking my hand in hers. Her fingers were warm and rough from years of performing, the pads stained faintly with ink.

"This place is full of people the world didn't want."

She guided my hand to the center of her chest, pressing my palm against the tattoo above her heart.

The ink pulsed faintly beneath my touch.

Alive.

Then her hand moved slightly, pulling aside a fold of fabric near her ribs.

There, glowing faintly in the firelight, was a tattoo I had never seen before.

It wasn't fully formed.

The shape resembled a swirl of smoke wrapped around a small flame. Thin tendrils stretched outward as though the design was still growing across her skin.

"This one," Lilith murmured, almost as if she hadn't meant to say it aloud, "appeared the night you arrived."

My breath caught.

"What?"

"I didn't understand it at first," she admitted quietly. "It burned when it appeared. Right here."

She touched the mark with two fingers.

"I thought it was a warning."

The smoke-shaped ink shifted faintly beneath her skin.

"Or a curse."

Her gaze lifted to mine.

"But then I saw you."

The small flame in the tattoo flickered.

"It stopped hurting," she said softly. "And I realized it wasn't a curse at all."

Her voice dropped into something quieter.

"It was you."

Tears stung unexpectedly at the corners of my eyes.

I glanced around the firepit.

No one was laughing anymore.

The performers watched with quiet understanding. Some nodded slightly, as though they had seen this sort of thing before. The Painted Man absently touched his throat where a faint new line of ink had begun to appear beneath his collar.

Sabine leaned closer to me, her voice warm against my ear.

"Now you understand."

Her hand rested lightly on my knee.

"We didn't choose the lives that broke us," she said. "But we survived them…and here we built something new from the wreckage."

The fire crackled softly.

The knot in my throat tightened.

"Freaks like me," I whispered.

Lilith shook her head gently.

"No," she said.

Her fingers tightened around mine.

"Freaks like us."

Chapter Twelve

Under the Big Top

Sabine Before the Fire

The fire cracked softly in the center of our circle, sending sparks spiraling into the dim rafters above the tent. Smoke drifted upward in slow, curling ribbons before disappearing into the dark canvas overhead. Most of dinner had been eaten hours ago, leaving behind only scattered crumbs of bread and bowls of soup growing cold in the night air. No one seemed eager to move, though. The circus had settled into one of its rare quiet moments, when the constant movement of rehearsal and preparation paused just long enough for everyone to breathe.

Sabine sat beside me with her legs folded beneath her, her eyes fixed on the fire as if it were whispering secrets only she could hear. She hadn't spoken much throughout the meal. While the others joked and passed wine around the circle, she had simply watched the flames with a distant look that made me wonder where her mind had wandered.

When she finally spoke, her voice came out low and steady.

"I lived in a village once."

The words slipped into the quiet like a blade through cloth.

"No name worth remembering," she continued. "I burned that name from every map and memory."

The conversation around the fire died instantly. Even the soft rustle of movement seemed to fade. Across the circle, Lilith's shifting tattoos slowed until they were nearly still, as though the ink itself was listening.

Sabine didn't look at me while she spoke, but I felt her words drawing me closer.

"I was born there," she said. "In a place where girls were taught to swallow their voices and stitch their shadows into the hems of their skirts. But I had something different under my skin. Fire. I didn't know it yet—not really. I only knew I felt… too much."

Her gaze softened as the flames reflected in her eyes.

Then the world shifted.

The scent of roasted vegetables and damp canvas faded away. In its place came the sharp smell of pine and woodsmoke. Cold air brushed across my face. Somewhere nearby, snow crunched beneath unseen footsteps.

I was still sitting beside Sabine.

And yet I wasn't.

The vision unfolded around me like a curtain lifting.

The village stood in a hollow between dark trees, its crooked houses leaning against one another as though they were tired of standing alone. The buildings were made of rough wood and packed mud, their chimneys coughing weak trails of smoke into the gray winter sky. Fog crept low across the ground, curling between fences and carts like a sleeping animal.

Snow dusted the rooftops.

Sabine stood a few steps ahead of me.

She was younger—sixteen at most. Her dark hair fell loose around her shoulders, tangled by the wind. A worn wool dress hung from her thin frame, the hem frayed from years of wear. Her bare feet pressed against the frostbitten grass as her breath rose in pale clouds before her face.

Her hands trembled slightly.

She darted between the houses with a book clutched tightly against her chest. Her cheeks were flushed from the cold, and her eyes shone with nervous excitement as she slipped through the narrow paths between buildings.

At the edge of the village stood a small chapel surrounded by crooked trees.

Behind it waited a grove.

And beneath one of those trees stood another girl.

Elinor.

The healer's apprentice.

She wore a simple apron tied around her waist, the fabric stained faintly green from crushed herbs. Even from a distance I could smell thyme and bitter bark clinging to her sleeves. Her hair was pulled back loosely, strands escaping to brush against her cheeks.

When she saw Sabine, her face softened instantly.

They didn't speak.

They didn't need to.

Sabine closed the distance between them in quick steps, and Elinor reached for her hands as though the movement had already been rehearsed a hundred times before. Their fingers intertwined naturally. Sabine leaned forward, pressing a quick, breathless kiss to Elinor's lips.

It was quiet.

Careful.

The kind of love that survives only in shadows.

They rested their foreheads together beneath the branches of the tree while the moon slipped through the leaves above them.

But secrets rarely stay hidden forever.

The vision shifted.

Days passed in the blink of an eye. Sabine grew taller. The softness in her face sharpened slightly, her watchful eyes always scanning the edges of the village as though she expected danger to come from the trees.

One night shouting shattered the quiet.

A cottage near the center of the village was surrounded by frightened voices. A woman sobbed loudly while a baby screamed somewhere inside the house. Villagers crowded around the doorway, their fear thick in the air.

Elinor pushed her way through them with quiet determination.

Inside the cottage, a small boy lay in a cradle, his face flushed with fever. Elinor knelt beside him immediately, pressing a cloth soaked in bitter-smelling herbs against his forehead. Her hands moved with calm confidence as she whispered something soothing to the child's mother.

Sabine stood just outside the doorway, her body tense.

"I dreamed of fire," she whispered urgently when Elinor stepped outside for fresh air. "Something is wrong. Don't go back in there."

Elinor smiled.

It was soft and steady, like moss growing beneath moonlight.

"I love you," she said gently.

She kissed Sabine's forehead.

Then she went back inside the house.

The child died before morning.

When Elinor came out everything had changed.

The villagers needed someone to blame.

They called her a witch.

They called Sabine her demon.

Her familiar.

Her corrupter.

They said they had seen Sabine wandering the woods at night, whispering to flames. They swore she walked through the snow without leaving footprints. They claimed she poisoned their wells and lured the healer's apprentice away from God.

It didn't matter what was true.

Fear only needs a story.

Rough hands dragged them both into the village square. I felt the ropes tighten around Sabine's wrists, biting into skin already raw from struggling. Cold stone pressed against our knees as villagers circled them with torches and furious prayers.

They tied Elinor to a wooden post.

The same people who once came to her for medicine now stacked wood around her feet.

Sabine didn't scream.

But something inside her shattered.

I felt the moment it happened.

The match struck.

Flames licked the base of the pyre.

But the fire did not rise the way it should have.

It moved sideways.

It turned.

The flames surged outward like a living creature, devouring the square in a wave of roaring heat. Houses ignited. Roofs collapsed. Villagers screamed as the fire raced through the narrow streets.

The inferno obeyed only one will.

Sabine's.

It spared no one.

Except her.

When the flames finally died, the village was nothing but ash.

Sabine lay curled in the blackened ruins, her dress burned away to ragged strips of cloth. Soot streaked her skin and hair while her chest rose and fell in shallow breaths.

She stared into nothing.

As if the girl she had been had burned away with the rest of the village.

Then a figure stepped out of the smoke.

Madame Thorne.

Her dark cloak moved gently in a wind that did not touch the ashes around her. She knelt beside Sabine and lifted the girl's scorched hands into her own.

"You will need to learn control," she said quietly.

Silver thread appeared in her fingers, glowing faintly as she wrapped it around Sabine's wrists.

"Power without guilt becomes tyranny," Thorne continued. "But guilt without growth is simply a slow death."

She helped Sabine to her feet.

And together they walked away from the ruins.

From the girl Sabine had been.

From the love she had lost.

From the village that no longer existed.

The vision shattered.

I gasped sharply as the world snapped back into place.

The firepit burned low again. The circus tents stood around us exactly as they had before. Crickets chirped somewhere in the grass, and distant laughter drifted across the camp.

Sabine sat beside me.

Watching.

"You saw it," she said quietly.

My throat tightened as I nodded.

"You saw her."

"Elinor," I whispered.

Sabine didn't answer with words.

But the grief inside her echoed through my chest like a second heartbeat.

I reached for her hand without thinking.

She let me take it.

"Do you still dream about her?" I asked softly.

Sabine remained silent.

She didn't need to speak.

Because I could still feel the ashes in her lungs.

The fire in her blood.

The hollow quiet that follows a life burned away.

Sabine didn't survive the fire.

She became it.

Chapter Thirteen

Under the Big Top

The Fire That Keeps

After Sabine's story, I couldn't sleep.

It wasn't only the horror of it—the burning village, the screaming crowds, the way grief had turned her magic into something unstoppable. What lingered in my chest was something stranger than fear. The air between us all had changed after she finished speaking, as though the truth had pulled something ancient from the shadows and now it refused to return to where it had been hiding.

The fire had burned low hours ago. Only a bed of glowing embers remained in the center of the camp, breathing faint orange light into the darkness. Most of the others had drifted back to their tents or vanished into the soft murmurs of the circus at midnight.

I stood outside my tent with my arms wrapped around myself, staring into the ash.

The quiet felt heavy.

Like the world was waiting.

I heard her before I saw her.

Sabine didn't walk the way other people did. She moved like the wind had decided where she belonged and simply carried her there—quiet, unhurried, wild in a way that made the night itself feel alive.

"You've got questions," she said.

Her voice came from the darkness beside the firepit.

"I do," I admitted.

Sabine crouched beside the dying fire and reached into the ash with bare fingers. When her skin touched the embers, they flared instantly, orange light licking up around her hand as if greeting an old friend. The flames curled along her palm without leaving so much as a mark.

Her skin glowed faintly.

As though something beneath it still burned.

"How are you still here?" I asked after a moment. My voice sounded small against the quiet of the night. "If that village—if Elinor—was hundreds of years ago… how are you still… you?"

Sabine let out a quiet laugh.

There was no humor in it.

"You think I haven't asked myself that question a thousand times?"

I didn't answer.

She turned slightly toward me, the firelight shifting across her face. In the glow she looked both younger and older than she had earlier that evening. The woman beside the fire was Sabine—but there was something ancient in the way she held herself.

Like time had passed through her without ever quite touching her.

"When Thorne found me," she said slowly, "I was barely alive. Not just from the fire. Not just from grief."

Her fingers sifted through the ash, stirring faint sparks.

"I had come undone."

She stared into the flames as if she could still see the ruins of the village there.

"Elinor was my anchor," she continued quietly. "My center. My reason to stay in the world. When they took her from me, something inside me unraveled. The fire didn't just burn the village that night."

Her voice softened.

"It burned the girl I used to be."

She picked up a small twig from the ground and rolled it between her fingers.

"Thorne didn't save me," Sabine said. "Not the way you're imagining. She didn't comfort me. She didn't promise things would get better."

She tossed the twig into the fire and watched it catch.

"She offered me a choice."

The word hung between us.

"What kind of choice?" I asked.

Sabine looked up at me then.

"To live," she said simply. "Not just as myself anymore—but as part of this. The circus. The family. The flame."

The twig snapped softly as it burned.

"When you choose it," she continued, "when you truly accept what this place is and what you are within it… the circus chooses you back."

A quiet shiver ran down my spine.

"That's why you haven't aged," I said slowly.

Sabine nodded.

"Once you cross that threshold," she explained, "once you stop fighting what you are and allow the circus to claim you… time stops moving the way it used to."

Her eyes drifted toward the tents around us.

"It still exists," she said. "It still passes. But it bends around the people who belong here."

"Is it immortality?" I asked.

Sabine shook her head gently.

"Not exactly. We can still bleed. We can still die. Pain still finds us when it wants to." She brushed ash from her hands and leaned back slightly. "Time simply forgets us."

The words settled deep in my chest.

I looked down at my hands, remembering the fire that had danced across my skin during the performance. The warmth that had answered Sabine's touch like it had always belonged to her.

"What happens if I don't choose it?" I asked quietly.

Sabine's eyes lifted to meet mine.

"Then the magic fades," she said.

Her voice held no judgment.

"Slowly, over time, the fire leaves your bones. The circus moves on to its next city, its next performers, its next stories." She shrugged slightly. "You go back to the world outside. You grow older. You live the life you were meant to have before you found us."

The thought twisted strangely in my chest.

"But if I do choose it?" I asked.

Sabine held my gaze for a long moment before answering.

"Then you never truly leave."

The fire crackled softly between us.

"The circus becomes your anchor," she continued. "Your blood. Your breath. We carry each other's burdens here. We protect one another. We become something larger than the lives we left behind."

Her voice lowered slightly.

"But it isn't just a life."

"What is it, then?"

"It's a vow."

The word felt heavier than the others.

"To what?" I asked.

Sabine reached toward me then, her fingers brushing lightly against my jaw. The warmth of her skin sent a quiet spark through my chest.

"To truth," she said softly.

Her thumb traced the edge of my cheek.

"No more hiding who you are. No more pretending you're smaller than the power inside you. No more shame."

Her voice dropped into something almost worshipful.

"Only fire."

The wind stirred the canvas tents behind us. Somewhere deeper in the circus grounds, a distant calliope began to play a slow, wandering tune that sounded like half a lullaby and half a ghost story.

"You're saying I'd become one of you," I said.

Sabine's expression softened.

"I'm saying you already are."

My heart pounded in my chest.

I thought of Thorne and her golden eyes. Of Lilith's living tattoos shifting beneath her skin. Of the beasts that bowed to their tamer in the ring. Of the girl who danced like smoke through the air without strings.

And I thought of my mother's voice echoing through cold church halls, scripture falling like stones against my skin while ice water burned down my scalp.

I had run away to escape that life.

But standing here beside the fire, I wondered if I had been running toward something all along.

"Is it forever?" I whispered.

Sabine's lips curved into the faintest smile.

"Only if you want it to be."

She extended her hand toward me.

The embers between us flared suddenly, rising into small twisting flames that moved with a strange, welcoming warmth instead of heat.

As if the fire itself had been waiting.

Slowly—without the fear that once lived inside me—I reached out and placed my hand in hers.

Chapter Fourteen

Before the Circus

The Breaking Point

It started long before the kiss.

Margaret and I had been stealing time together for weeks—small moments hidden in the quiet corners of town where no one thought to look too closely. Notes slipped beneath hymnals during Sunday service. Fingers brushing beneath the table during afternoon tea. The quick, electric thrill of her shoulder pressing against mine when we walked side by side down the church aisle.

Something sacred lived between us.

Even if everyone else would have called it sin.

Margaret was the pastor's niece. She had come to live with her uncle after her parents died the winter before. People in town spoke about her with a kind of gentle pity, describing her as sweet and quiet and obedient. They said it the way people spoke about lambs—soft creatures meant to be protected.

But when Margaret looked at me, there was nothing soft about it.

There was fire.

We weren't foolish enough to believe we could hide forever. Every glance, every touch, every whispered word carried the weight of risk. But we were seventeen, and the world had not yet managed to crush the stubborn hope living inside our chests.

And we were in love.

That night we met behind the chapel again.

The ivy along the stone walls rustled softly in the wind, and the stars hung low above the trees like lanterns scattered across the sky. Margaret was already waiting when I arrived, her back pressed against the cool brick of the building.

The moment she saw me, her entire face lit up.

"You came," she whispered.

"Of course I did."

She reached for me immediately, pulling me close until I could feel the warmth of her body through the thin fabric of our dresses. Her hands slipped around my waist, steady and certain, and for a moment the entire world seemed to fall away.

We sank down into the grass behind the chapel where no one could see us.

Margaret pulled me gently into her lap, her arms wrapping around me as if she had been waiting all day to hold me like that. I leaned back against her chest, listening to the quiet rhythm of her breathing while the cool night air brushed against our skin.

"Sometimes I think we should just leave," she murmured softly.

My heart skipped.

"Leave where?"

"Anywhere," she said. "Somewhere people don't watch every step we take."

Her fingers threaded through mine.

"Somewhere we could be… us."

The words settled deep inside my chest, warm and dangerous.

I turned toward her, and our mouths found each other in the quiet darkness.

The kiss was soft at first—hesitant, searching—but the longer it lasted, the more desperate it became. Our whispers tangled together between breaths, promises spoken too quickly and too quietly to survive the light of day.

I didn't hear my mother's footsteps on the stone path.

Not until it was too late.

Her scream split the night open.

"You disgusting, vile little creatures!"

Margaret's hands vanished from my waist instantly. She pushed me away as though I had burned her, scrambling to her feet with trembling fingers as she fumbled to fasten the buttons of her blouse.

For one terrible moment our eyes met.

Then she ran.

I watched her disappear down the path, her pale dress vanishing into the darkness beyond the churchyard.

Part of me hated her for leaving.

Another part hated myself for wanting her to stay.

My mother said nothing as she grabbed my wrist.

Her grip was so tight it made my bones ache. She dragged me down the stone path toward home without speaking a single word. The silence between us was worse than any shouting could have been.

Inside the house, she shoved me forward so hard that I fell to the floor.

Then she threw something toward me and it struck my chest.

A folded letter.

"They're expecting you," she said coldly. "You should thank me."

My hands trembled as I opened it.

The words blurred together at first, but one name stood out clearly enough to freeze the air in my lungs.

St. Vincent's Restoration Home for Girls.

I read the rest in fragments.

Reform.

Moral guidance.

Path to purity.

"I'm not going," I said quietly.

My mother didn't even look up from where she stood beside the table.

"Yes," she said. "You are."

I crumpled the paper in my fist.

"This is a prison."

"No," she snapped sharply. "This is a blessing. A chance to scrub the disease out of your soul before you rot in hell."

"You think this is what God wants?" I demanded, my voice shaking. "You think God is proud of what you're doing?"

Her hand struck my face before I finished the sentence.

The force of it snapped my head sideways. Pain exploded across my mouth as the taste of blood filled my throat.

"You lay with another girl," she hissed. "In God's house."

Her eyes burned with something darker than anger.

"That wasn't just sin, Evelyn. That was defilement."

I pushed myself up from the floor, my chest heaving.

"You are unclean."

Something inside me snapped then.

I don't remember exactly what I screamed. I only remember the sound tearing out of my throat, wild and broken. I knocked something off the table as I stumbled backward—maybe a cup, maybe a vase.

It shattered against the floor.

My mother grabbed my hair.

The pain yanked my head back as she dragged me down the hallway toward the cellar door.

The steps were cold beneath me as she shoved me down into the darkness below.

Rope waited there.

She tied my wrists behind my back with practiced efficiency, pulling the knot so tight it made my fingers numb. Then she shoved me into the corner of the cellar like I was something she had already thrown away.

"You'll wait here," she said, "until the men arrive."

The door closed.

Above me, I could hear her kneel.

Her voice rose in prayer, loud and steady.

"Burn away the wickedness," she said. "Cleanse her with fire and ice. Let her flesh remember the wages of sin."

Her voice never trembled.

Mine did.

I sat in the darkness with the cold dirt pressing through my dress and thought a single terrible thing.

This is how girls disappear.

Time lost its meaning down there. The only thing I could measure were the prayers drifting through the floorboards above me.

Then came the knock.

Calm.

Professional.

Two men stepped into the cellar a few minutes later, their shoes clean despite the dirt floor. They wore dark suits and thin leather gloves, the kind of men who carried God in their pockets like paperwork.

"She's ready," my mother said from the doorway.

One of the men crouched in front of me.

His smile was polite.

Empty.

"You'll be safe now, Miss Evelyn," he said gently. "We're going to help you start fresh."

He untied the rope around my wrists.

Pain rushed through my hands as blood returned to my fingers in sharp bursts of heat. For a moment I simply sat there, staring at my hands like they belonged to someone else.

Then I realized what I had to do. I pushed him away.

I ran.

Up the cellar stairs.

Past my mother.

Through the front door.

The cold night air struck my face as I tore across the yard and into the forest beyond the house. Branches clawed at my dress as I stumbled through the trees, my journal clutched against my chest like it was the only thing anchoring me to the world.

I didn't stop running.

Not until the house disappeared behind me.

Not until the trees swallowed me whole.

And then—

Somewhere in the distance—

I heard music.

Chapter Fifteen

Under the Big Top

The Mirror Tent

The tent was quiet.

Not silent—nothing in the circus was ever truly silent—but hushed in a way that made the air feel reverent, as though the space itself understood it held something sacred.

From the outside it didn't look like much. The canvas was pale and soft against the moonlight, rippling faintly whenever the night wind brushed across it. It was smaller than most of the other tents, tucked between two towering striped structures like a forgotten thought.

If you didn't know what it was, you might have walked past it without a second glance.

But something about it pulled at me.

The entrance flap hung open just slightly, the canvas shifting back and forth in a slow breath.

Waiting.

I stepped inside.

The world changed.

The temperature warmed instantly, wrapping around my skin like the quiet comfort of a hearth. The cool bite of the night air vanished behind me, replaced by something softer—something fragrant.

Lavender.

Eucalyptus.

Old polished wood.

The scents drifted together like a memory I couldn't quite place.

Then I saw them.

Mirrors.

Dozens.

Hundreds.

They filled the tent from floor to ceiling, layered upon one another in an endless maze of glass and reflection. Some were tall and elegant with carved wooden frames curling like vines around the edges. Others were small and circular, suspended from thin silver chains that swayed gently whenever I moved.

A few were cracked.

Others warped the reflections in strange ways, bending light like water rippling over stone.

The deeper I stepped into the tent, the more mirrors appeared, angled carefully so that each reflection opened into another corridor of glass.

It should have felt overwhelming.

Instead it felt… familiar.

Like walking into a dream I had already lived.

The first mirror caught my attention almost immediately.

I stepped toward it slowly.

The girl staring back at me looked exactly the way I remembered myself just weeks ago—pale and nervous, shoulders pulled inward as though I expected the world to strike me at any moment. My eyes darted toward the edges of the reflection like a trapped animal waiting for a door to open.

Even through the glass I could feel the weight she carried.

Fear.

Shame.

The constant need to be smaller than the space around her.

I moved on.

The next mirror showed a younger version of me.

My hair was pulled painfully tight against my scalp, each strand pinned into place the way my mother demanded. My back was straight, my posture rigid with obedience.

I recognized the look in my eyes instantly.

Desperation.

The quiet, aching need to be good enough.

Another mirror waited nearby.

I almost walked past it before the reflection inside made me stop.

This version of me looked different.

Older.

Stronger.

She wore black lace that curled around her body like smoke, the fabric shifting with each small movement. Firelight danced in her palms, glowing gold and red against the darkness of the tent behind her.

But it wasn't the fire that startled me.

It was her expression.

She wasn't afraid.

She looked at me the way someone looks at their own reflection after surviving something terrible—steady, certain, unashamed.

Slowly, I lifted my hand.

The other Evelyn lifted hers too.

Our fingertips hovered inches apart on opposite sides of the glass.

"You're beginning to see."

The voice came from behind me.

I turned.

Madame Thorne stood inside one of the mirrors near the edge of the tent.

For a moment I simply stared.

This reflection of her was not quite the same woman who led the circus.

Her gown shimmered like a night sky, tiny stars woven into the fabric so that they seemed to flicker with quiet light. Her hair flowed freely around her shoulders, silver strands moving as though touched by a wind that did not exist in the tent.

And her eyes—

They shimmered with gold, red, and soft bush tones, deep and endless like the sky moments before the sun surrenders to night.

"See what?" I asked softly.

Thorne stepped forward.

The surface of the mirror rippled as though it had turned to water. The glass bent around her as she passed through it, then smoothed again once she stood beside me.

"The paths not taken," she said gently.

Her gaze drifted toward the mirrors surrounding us.

"The selves you buried because someone told you they were wrong."

She gestured lightly toward the reflections.

"The ones you fear."

Then her voice softened.

"And the ones you have not yet allowed yourself to become."

I turned slowly.

The mirrors had changed.

In one reflection I stood in the center of the chapel beside Margaret. Our hands were entwined openly, our fingers laced together without hesitation while the congregation whispered and stared around us.

Margaret looked happy.

So did I.

Another mirror showed something darker.

I stood across from my mother in the small kitchen of our house. I was older now, my shoulders relaxed, my expression calm. My mother looked smaller somehow, her sharp anger dulled by time.

The look in my eyes was impossible to read.

Forgiveness.

Or pity.

Or something colder still.

"How is this possible?" I whispered.

"This is the Mirror Tent," Thorne replied.

Her voice carried the quiet weight of something ancient.

"It does not show the present alone. It reveals what was… what might have been… and what still lives quietly beneath the surface of your soul."

She walked slowly through the maze of glass, her reflection multiplying endlessly in the mirrors around us.

"Every member of this circus stands here eventually," she continued. "It is how we come to understand each other—not through lies or performance, but through truth."

Her eyes found mine again.

"And now you stand here too."

The mirrors shifted once more.

New visions appeared across the silver surfaces.

I saw Lilith younger, her hands shaking as blood dripped from her fingers while the first lines of living ink crawled across her skin. Her eyes were wide with horror and wonder as the tattoos took root.

Another mirror showed Sabine kneeling in ash before a burning pyre, her grief so fierce it bent the fire itself around her body.

Another.

Marionette.

Before the strings.

Before the circus.

Before something had hollowed her out and rebuilt her into the girl who danced above the crowd.

The images flickered across the mirrors like stolen memories.

I staggered back.

"I don't want to see this."

Thorne's expression softened.

"But you already have."

She stepped closer.

"This tent does not create these truths," she said gently. "It simply reveals them."

Her hand lifted slightly, hovering near my shoulder without touching.

"These stories live inside the people you now call family."

My chest tightened.

"I'm not like my mother," I whispered.

The words felt fragile.

"I need to know that."

Thorne's gaze sharpened.

"You are nothing like that woman."

Her voice carried the quiet strength of iron wrapped in velvet.

"She used fear to control the world around her."

Her eyes softened.

"You survived it."

A mirror beside us cracked softly.

The sound was delicate, like ice breaking across the surface of a frozen lake.

The fractured glass shifted.

A new reflection appeared.

It was me.

I stood in the center of the circus ring wearing a plum and silver costume that shimmered like smoke under lantern light. The crowd beyond the ring gasped as fire spiraled from my fingertips, rising into the air like living ribbons.

But the girl in the mirror didn't look frightened.

She looked powerful.

She looked free.

"You get to choose who you become now," Thorne said quietly.

The words settled deep inside my chest.

I took a slow breath.

Then another.

The mirrors around me shimmered as though the tent itself was watching.

Waiting.

And finally—

I stepped forward.

Chapter Sixteen

Under the Big Top

Ash and Lanterns

When I finally stepped out of the Mirror Tent, the night felt different.

Not colder. Not darker. Just sharper somehow, as if the world had been cleaned of its softer edges while I stood among all that glass. The circus stretched around me in flickers of gold and crimson, lanterns swaying gently between ropes and poles while distant music drifted low across the grounds. For a moment I simply stood there with one hand still resting against the flap behind me, trying to steady the strange ache inside my chest.

The mirrors had not frightened me in the way I expected.

They had done something worse.

They had shown me pieces of myself I could no longer pretend not to recognize.

I let the flap fall shut behind me and started walking without any real destination in mind. The paths between the tents curled through the encampment like winding veins, packed dirt soft beneath my boots, the edges silvered by moonlight. Somewhere nearby, someone laughed in a voice so bright it sounded like breaking glass. Somewhere else, something howled—not in pain, but in a way that made the hair rise gently along my arms.

The circus never truly rested. Even now, deep into the night, it breathed around me.

A woman sat at a small wooden table beneath a crooked lantern, her sleeves rolled to the elbow. At first I thought she was simply sewing. Then the needle slipped clean through the skin of her palm. She didn't flinch. Crimson welled for only a heartbeat before the wound sealed itself as though the flesh had never been broken at all. Around her feet lay scraps of cloth stitched into strange little shapes—birds, foxes, things with too many legs. When she finished the final stitch on one of them, she set it gently on the ground. The cloth creature twitched once... then scurried into the shadows.

Further on, a man in a velvet waistcoat sat beside an open wagon, shuffling a deck of cards between long pale fingers. Every time he flicked one into the air, it turned briefly into a white moth before landing back in his hand as paper again. He didn't look up as I passed, though one of the cards drifted toward me on its own, brushing against my sleeve before fluttering harmlessly to the ground.

I bent to pick it up.

The face of the card was blank.

When I looked up again, the man was smiling to himself as though he had heard a joke I hadn't.

I kept walking.

Near the far edge of camp, a girl with no shoes and hair the color of candlewax sat cross-legged in the grass, whispering to three tiny flames that danced in a circle around her knees. They dipped and spun obediently, rising and falling with each word she spoke. On the roof of the next wagon over, a black cat with two tails watched her with solemn yellow eyes.

Everywhere I looked there was something strange.

Something beautiful.

Something that should have felt impossible and yet did not.

That was what unnerved me most.

The circus was becoming familiar.

I found myself near the animal wagons. The air there was warmer, thick with hay and fur and the musky sweetness of living things. A low rumble came from somewhere in the shadows, followed by the soft clink of chain and the rustle of something large shifting in its sleep. I paused beside one of the wagons and looked through the slats.

Inside, a creature lay curled in the straw beneath a hanging lantern. At first glance it looked like a lioness. Then it lifted its head, and I saw the long, curling horns sweeping back from its skull and the dark mane braided with thin red ribbons. It blinked once, slow and golden, before settling its head back onto its paws.

"You get used to that eventually."

I turned at the sound of Sabine's voice.

She stood a few feet away with her arms folded loosely across her chest, one shoulder propped against the wheel of a nearby wagon. Firelight from a hanging lantern warmed the planes of her face, catching in the dark waves of her hair. Tonight she wore no performance costume, only a loose shirt laced carelessly at the throat and dark trousers tucked into worn boots. Even dressed simply, she looked like something made from heat and shadow.

"I'm not sure that makes me feel better," I admitted.

Sabine smiled faintly and pushed away from the wagon. "That one's harmless," she said, nodding toward the horned lioness. "Mostly."

"Mostly?"

"She only bit Lucien twice."

I laughed before I could stop myself.

The sound surprised both of us.

Sabine's expression softened at it, and suddenly I became painfully aware of how close she was standing. There was always something unsettling about that with her—not because she frightened me, but because she didn't. My body seemed to know her before my mind had time to decide what to do with that knowledge.

"You disappeared after the Mirror Tent," she said.

I looked away toward the wagon slats. "I didn't mean to."

"You don't have to explain." Her voice was quieter now. "People usually leave that tent carrying more than they brought in."

I thought of the reflections. Margaret. My mother. The girl in the ring with fire in her hands and no fear left in her face.

"It showed me things I didn't ask to see," I said.

Sabine stepped beside me and rested her forearms against the wagon rail, looking in at the sleeping creature as if the conversation didn't need to be looked at directly either.

"That's what it does."

A breeze moved through the camp, stirring the loose strands of her hair. I caught the smell of smoke on her skin again, mixed now with the faint spice of clove and something darker I couldn't name.

"Did it frighten you," I asked, "the first time you went in?"

Sabine was silent for a moment. "Yes," she said at last. "But not because of what it showed me. Because of how badly I wanted some of it to be true."

I turned to look at her.

She was already watching me.

The heat that passed between us then was quieter than the fire she carried, but no less dangerous.

Before I could say anything, another presence moved at the edge of my vision.

Lilith stepped between the lanterns as if she had been carved out of the dark itself. She wore a black silk robe loose over one shoulder, its hem dragging softly over the ground, and her tattoos caught the light in restless flashes as she approached. Some of the ink along her collarbone shifted as she moved, a vine unfurling lazily beneath her skin before settling again.

"So this is where you vanished to," she said, her voice rich with amusement.

Sabine's mouth twitched at one corner. "She was admiring the locals."

Lilith's gaze flicked to the horned lioness, then back to me. "A wise choice. They're easier than people."

She came to stand on my other side, not touching, but close enough that the silk of her sleeve brushed lightly against my hand before falling away. If Sabine's nearness felt like warmth gathering in my chest, Lilith's felt like standing at the edge of deep water and wanting, against all reason, to step in.

"You look shaken," she said.

"The Mirror Tent," Sabine answered for me.

Lilith hummed softly, as if that explained everything. "It tends to leave teeth marks."

"I'm beginning to think every part of this place does," I muttered.

That won another small smile from Sabine, and Lilith laughed outright.

The sound of it slid over me, dark and smooth.

For a little while, the three of us stood there in a silence that did not feel empty. Around us, the circus moved in its midnight rhythm. Somewhere across the grounds, a burst of blue sparks rose into the air and hovered like a cluster of stars before drifting slowly downward. A woman passed carrying a tray of glass bottles filled with tiny storms, each one flashing faintly with distant lightning. In the next row of tents, someone began to sing in a language I did not know, and one by one, the lanterns nearest us brightened as if leaning closer to hear.

Lilith followed my gaze to the bottles of lightning and said, almost absently, "Do you know what I like most about this place?"

I shook my head.

"That no one asks you to be less strange to make them comfortable."

The words hit me with surprising force.

Sabine's hand brushed mine, just once, a contact so light I might have imagined it if the warmth had not lingered afterward.

"You don't have to understand everything all at once," she said quietly. "The circus doesn't ask that of you."

Lilith tipped her head, studying me with those impossible violet eyes. "It only asks whether you're brave enough to keep looking."

I thought of the mirrors again. Of the selves I had buried. Of the selves still waiting.

"Maybe I'm trying," I said.

Sabine's expression softened into something almost tender. "That's enough for now."

For reasons I could not fully explain, those words loosened something inside me.

Not all at once.

Just enough.

The three of us drifted back toward the heart of the encampment together, not in any formal way, not with hands clasped or promises spoken aloud, but with a quiet sense of orbit—as though each of us had stepped into the gravity of the others without quite meaning to.

When we passed the firepit, I stopped.

The embers had burned low, but now and then a thread of orange still moved beneath the ash. On impulse, I crouched and stretched my hand toward the dying glow. Heat stirred faintly beneath my skin in answer, and one of the embers brightened.

Then another.

A tiny flame rose, no bigger than the tip of my finger.

I stared at it, breath caught.

Sabine crouched beside me, close enough that her knee brushed mine. Lilith remained standing above us, her robe whispering in the night wind.

"You see?" Sabine said softly. "It's listening now."

The little flame trembled, then steadied.

I should have been afraid of how easily it answered me.

Instead I felt something else.

Not power, exactly.

Not yet.

Possibility.

I glanced up at them—at Sabine with her quiet, banked warmth, and Lilith with her knowing half-shadow smile—and since stepping into the circus I understood that belonging was not one single moment. It was made of smaller ones. A shared silence. A hand nearly touching yours. Someone finding you after you'd been lost in your own head and not asking you to explain before they stayed.

The flame danced once more across my fingertips before sinking gently back into the embers.

When I stood, Lilith was still watching me.

"So," she said, her lips curving. "The girl in smoke glows after midnight."

Heat climbed into my face.

Sabine laughed under her breath.

And together, beneath the low lantern light and the breathing dark of the circus, we walked on.

Chapter Seventeen

Under the Big Top

The Moth Girl

I tried to stay away from the Mirror Tent. But the circus has a way of calling you toward the truths you aren't ready to face.

I hadn't meant to return. I told myself I would sleep, that I would let the strange visions from the night before settle into something manageable. But the longer I lay in my cot, the more the memory of the mirrors tugged at the edges of my mind.

They didn't simply reflect.

They breathed.

Like lungs slowly filling with air.

By the time the moon climbed high enough to silver the canvas roofs of the circus, I found myself walking back toward the pale tent without remembering the moment I chose to leave my bed.

The entrance flap was already open.

Waiting.

Inside, the air wrapped around me again—warm, fragrant, alive with the quiet perfume of lavender and polished wood. The mirrors stretched endlessly in every direction, catching the lantern light in fractured glimmers that moved whenever I did.

This time, I walked deeper.

Past the reflections that showed me as a child kneeling in church pews. Past the version of myself cloaked in smoke and fire that still watched me with calm, knowing eyes. Past another mirror where my face had sharpened into something colder, something almost dangerous.

Each step seemed to open another corridor of glass.

Then I saw her.

At first it was only movement in the reflection.

Something pale.

Something trembling.

I turned toward the mirror and froze.

Wings.

They spread wide behind the figure inside the glass, delicate and veined like pressed petals trapped beneath ice. The thin membranes shimmered faintly as they moved, each fragile ripple catching the lantern light in ghostly colors.

The girl beneath them stood perfectly still.

Her skin was pale enough to look almost translucent, the faint blue veins beneath it tracing delicate paths along her neck and temples. Her lips held the faintest tint of blue, as though winter had never quite left her body.

The Moth Girl.

She stared at me through the mirror.

Before I could speak, the glass began to ripple.

The surface of the mirror softened, bending inward like water disturbed by a falling stone.

The Moth Girl stepped forward.

Not into the tent.

But through the mirror and into me, I was no longer Evelyn, I had become Clara.

The cold hit first.

A deep, bone-aching cold that seemed to settle into my lungs the moment I tried to breathe.

London.

1814.

The winter had frozen the city solid.

The Thames had turned to ice so thick that merchants dragged carts across its surface. The wind howled through narrow streets, rattling shutters and turning every breath into frost.

I stood in a dim basement room.

The air smelled of iron.

And chemicals.

And something far worse.

"My daughter will be remembered," a man's voice said somewhere behind me. "History rewards those who dare to ask impossible questions."

I turned.

My father.

He had once been a respected doctor. His name had filled medical journals and lecture halls. People once trusted his hands to heal them.

But something inside him had twisted.

Obsession had hollowed him out and replaced everything human with curiosity.

He believed in transformation.

In evolution forced through suffering.

In the idea that death itself might be overcome if someone were brave enough to experiment long enough.

And I was his experiment.

I was six when the surgeries began.

At first he called them improvements.

"You're special Clara," he whispered as he prepared his tools. "You were born for this."

The basement walls were thick stone, the kind that swallowed screams before they could reach the street above. A narrow iron bed sat beneath a hanging lamp whose light flickered whenever the wind rattled the house above.

He worked slowly.

Carefully.

Like a sculptor shaping clay.

Delicate bones—thin as bird skeletons—were sewn into my shoulder blades. He carved long slits along my back where something new could grow.

I screamed until my throat tore open.

The neighbors never heard.

The pain never ended.

At night he injected poisons into my veins to see how long I could survive them. Mercury. Belladonna. Arsenic diluted with laudanum to quiet my convulsions. Every reaction was written neatly into a red leather notebook he kept beside the furnace.

"You're surviving things no one else could," he murmured once as fever burned through my body. "You're extraordinary."

My wings grew slowly.

At first they were wrong.

Thin and wet like torn parchment.

He cut them away.

And began again.

I don't know how many times he tried.

Eventually they stayed.

The wings shimmered faintly beneath the dim lantern light, delicate veins glowing faint silver as they stretched across my back.

My father cried when he saw them.

Not because I was in pain.

Because his experiment had succeeded.

But the wings hurt.

Every movement sent fresh agony through my shoulders as they scraped against the walls of the iron cage where he kept me. Infection burned through my veins while the fragile membranes tore and healed and tore again.

I wasn't the only one in the basement.

Other cages lined the walls.

Other children.

Other experiments.

Other failures.

One boy's skin had turned thin and translucent, his organs visible beneath the surface like glass sculptures. Another girl had grown an extra jaw that hung uselessly beneath her chin.

They didn't live long.

None of them did.

Their screams faded one by one.

Eventually the basement grew quiet.

Except for me.

After a while I stopped crying.

But inside my mind—

I screamed.

And something heard me.

At first it was only a sound.

A soft humming that threaded through the fever burning behind my eyes. It felt ancient, older than the city above us, older than the world that had built these walls.

Then the voice came.

Not spoken aloud.

But clear as thought.

I see you.

The basement door never opened.

Yet suddenly she was there.

Madame Thorne knelt beside the cage as though she had always been meant to find me there. Her dark cloak brushed the floor as she reached through the bars and pressed her cool fingers against my temple.

"My god," she whispered, her voice trembling. "What has he done to you?"

For the first time in years—

I answered someone.

Not with words.

But with a thought that burned through my mind.

Help me.

She lifted me from the cage as though I weighed nothing.

The moment her arms wrapped around me, the pain began to fade. The iron bars, the stone walls, the furnace—all of it blurred like a nightmare dissolving in daylight.

We vanished.

I never saw the basement again.

I never saw my father again either.

I don't know what Madame Thorne did after she carried me away.

I have never asked.

But I know this much.

He never touched another child again.

The mirrors shimmered.

The cold vanished.

I staggered forward as the vision collapsed around me, I was Evelyn again.

The warm air of the circus returned to my lungs in a rush as the Mirror Tent reformed around my body. My knees nearly buckled as I tried to steady myself.

Across the glass corridor stood the Moth Girl.

Her wings brushed the air softly behind her like rustling paper.

"You saw it," she said.

My throat felt tight.

"That man… your father?"

She nodded once.

"He gave me these wings," she said quietly.

Her fingers brushed the delicate veins stretched across them.

"And I wear them as a warning."

The mirrors behind her flickered.

For a moment I saw flashes of the past again—needles, notebooks, cages filled with shadows.

Then the images changed.

The same wings stretched wide against an open sky.

Sunlight poured through their delicate membranes as she lifted into the air above the circus tents.

Free.

"You survived," I whispered.

She shook her head gently.

"I escaped."

Her gaze drifted toward the mirrors surrounding us.

"Thorne didn't just save my life," she said. "She answered a call I didn't even know I was sending."

The tent grew very still.

Slowly, I reached out and touched the edge of one of her wings.

The surface shimmered beneath my fingertips, faint symbols etched along the fragile veins like runes carved into glass.

One of them caught the light.

For a moment I thought it spelled a single word.

Mercy.

"I'm glad she found you," I said quietly.

The Moth Girl nodded.

"So am I."

Her wings folded gently behind her.

Then she stepped backward into the mirrors.

The glass rippled once more, swallowing her reflection until only the endless maze of silver remained.

I stood alone in the tent again.

The mirrors stretched endlessly around me, quiet and patient.

How many stories lived inside them?

How many broken girls stood where I stood now, staring at the ghosts of who they used to be?

Somewhere beyond the glass, the circus breathed in the dark.

Waiting for me.

Chapter Eighteen

Under the Big Top

The Painted Man

The Mirror Tent let me go slowly.

It felt almost reluctant, as if the mirrors themselves were unwilling to release me back into the ordinary rhythm of the circus. When I finally stepped outside, the cool evening air struck my face and I realized my legs were trembling.

The Moth Girl's memories still echoed inside my chest. The cold basement. The rustling wings. The quiet moment when Madame Thorne had carried her out of the dark.

For a long moment I stood there beneath the lantern light, trying to steady my breathing.

The circus had grown quieter.

Not empty—never empty—but hushed in that strange hour before the night performance began. Somewhere in the distance someone tuned a violin, the sharp notes cutting through the evening air like threads of silver. The ropes of the high wire creaked faintly as a performer tested their tension. Voices murmured behind velvet curtains.

The calm before the spectacle.

The calm before the masks went on and the lights burned bright enough to hide every scar.

I began walking without thinking.

The sounds of the circus guided me through the maze of tents—past the animal enclosures, past the supply wagons, past a pair of acrobats practicing silent flips beneath a lantern. My mind drifted somewhere between exhaustion and wonder, still tangled in the strange gravity of the Mirror Tent.

That was when I saw him.

The Painted Man sat alone near the back of the performers' tent.

A worn wooden bench held his weight, its legs slightly crooked in the dirt. The lantern above him burned low, leaving half his body swallowed by shadow. His coat hung over the back of the bench, leaving his arms bare to the night air.

Even from a distance, his tattoos moved.

Not violently.

Not like living creatures.

More like restless dreams shifting beneath skin.

Tiny figures crept slowly across his forearms. Symbols slid along his shoulders like drifting clouds. The ink shimmered faintly whenever the lantern light flickered.

He hadn't noticed me yet.

Or perhaps he had and simply didn't care.

For a moment I considered turning away. Performers guarded their solitude fiercely before a show. It was the last quiet moment before they stepped into the ring and became someone else.

But something held me there.

Maybe it was the movement beneath his skin.

Maybe it was the expression on his face—distant, thoughtful, like a man who had already wandered somewhere far away from the circus.

Or maybe I was beginning to understand something about this place.

No one ended up here by accident.

Every performer carried a story.

Every story began with a breaking point.

I stepped closer.

The Painted Man lifted his head before I could speak.

His eyes were pale—almost gray—but thin lines of ink curled faintly at their edges, like veins of shadow beneath the surface of his skin. He studied me quietly, the way a reader studies a page before deciding whether the words are worth their time.

"You shouldn't be back here," he said finally.

His voice was low and rough, like gravel sliding beneath water.

"Most people avoid this side of the tent before a show," he continued. "It tends to… stir things."

"I don't think I'm like most people," I replied softly.

The corner of his mouth twitched.

It might have been a smile.

Or just the ghost of one.

I sat beside him, leaving enough space between us to respect the quiet he seemed to value.

Up close, the tattoos were even more unsettling.

They weren't simply images.

They moved, similar to Lilith's, but somehow different at the same time.

A woman walked slowly backward along the inside of his wrist. A burning house flickered faintly on his forearm, its smoke drifting toward his elbow. Near his shoulder, two wolves circled endlessly, their tails twisting into their own mouths.

"You were in the Mirror Tent," he said.

It wasn't a question.

I nodded.

"Did it show you who you are?"

"It showed me who I might become," I answered. "And who I've been trying not to become."

He was silent for a moment.

Then he spoke again.

"Mine don't live in glass."

His fingers brushed lightly across the shifting ink on his arm.

"They live in flesh."

He turned his forearm toward me.

"Touch one."

I hesitated.

The movement beneath the ink had grown slower now, almost watchful.

"They only reveal themselves to people who already know what it means to carry something heavy," he said quietly.

Slowly, I reached out.

My fingertips brushed the image of a small door drawn at the center of his forearm.

The moment I touched it—

The circus vanished.

Rain.

Cold.

Relentless.

Mud clung to my feet as though it wanted to drag me back into the earth.

He was younger.

The Painted Man—before the circus, before the ink had spread across his body like a second skin. His ribs pressed sharply against his thin frame as he stood barefoot in the mud, chains hanging from his wrists.

The shackles weren't meant to hold him.

They were meant to humiliate him.

He had been captured during a war he never intended to fight. Dragged from his village by soldiers who needed bodies more than they needed reasons.

But the worst part wasn't the prison.

It was the guilt.

"I lied," his voice echoed through the rain.

He had given them a name.

Another man's name.

A rebel hiding in the hills.

He had done it to save his own life.

But the soldiers branded him a traitor anyway.

They dragged him to a place they called the Ink House.

It stood at the edge of the prison camp, its doors painted with elaborate symbols meant to disguise the truth of what happened inside.

It was a torture chamber.

Dressed up like art.

Inside waited a man wearing deep red robes.

He carried needles carved from bone.

The first mark went into the Painted Man's back.

It cut like any blade.

But the pain burned deeper than flesh.

They weren't just drawing pictures.

They were forcing stories into him.

Every confession—true or false—became a mark.

A girl he had loved and abandoned.

A coin he had once stolen.

A soldier he was accused of killing.

Each story carved itself into his skin.

Each image moved.

Each one whispered.

After a while he stopped remembering which stories were his.

I gasped and pulled my hand away.

The circus returned all at once—the lantern light, the smell of sawdust, the distant music drifting from the main tent.

The Painted Man flexed his fingers slowly.

The tattoos settled again.

"You're cursed," I said softly.

He didn't answer immediately.

"Some of them are true," he said eventually.

His voice carried no bitterness.

"Some of them aren't. But once the ink entered my skin, truth stopped mattering."

"How did you escape?" I asked.

His mouth twitched again.

"I didn't."

He pulled back the collar of his shirt slightly.

At the base of his neck was a single mark unlike the others.

A black spade.

Sharp.

Simple.

"The last mark they gave me was a death sentence," he said. "They left me in the woods with the rest of the condemned. My body was covered in stories I could no longer separate from myself."

His eyes softened slightly.

"That was the night she found me."

"Thorne," I said.

He nodded.

"She said the ink was screaming," he murmured. "That the stories were howling through my skin like wolves."

His fingers brushed lightly across his arm again.

"She didn't recoil when the tattoos moved," he said quietly. "She didn't try to erase them."

The lantern light shifted across the ink.

"She told me that if I wanted to live, I needed to choose something larger than the pain."

"And you chose the circus."

"No," he said.

He looked directly at me.

"I chose to live."

A pause.

"And the circus accepted the choice."

He stood slowly, pulling his sleeves back down over the restless ink beneath his skin.

The music from the main tent had grown louder.

The show was about to begin.

"Remember something," he said as he turned toward the curtain.

"What?"

"Don't touch more than one story at a time."

He glanced back at me briefly.

"The ink has limits."

Then his voice dropped slightly.

"But your mind does too."

He disappeared into the darkness of the performers' entrance.

I sat alone for a long moment, staring at the empty space he had left behind.

And I couldn't decide which part of him was more dangerous.

The ink.

Or the man strong enough to survive it.

Chapter Nineteen

Under the Big Top

The Story They Told

The next town sat two days down the road.

We arrived just before sunset, the wagons rolling into the open field that had been cleared for traveling performers and livestock traders. The air smelled of damp earth and pine sap, and the sky above the hills burned orange as the sun sank behind the trees.

Setting up the circus always felt like watching a strange creature assemble itself.

Ropes rose first.

Then poles.

Then canvas.

Within an hour the empty field had transformed into something alive—striped tents rising like giant flowers from the dirt while lanterns flickered awake one by one across the grounds. The animals were led into their enclosures, the musicians tuned their instruments, and the scent of roasted nuts drifted from a small cart near the entrance gate.

The circus breathed.

And I breathed with it.

I was helping Sabine carry a crate of glass bottles toward the performers' tent when I heard the voices.

Two men stood near the edge of the grounds beside a supply wagon. They weren't part of the circus. Their coats were too stiff, their boots too clean. Townsfolk.

Traveling shows always drew curious eyes before the first performance.

One of them leaned against the wagon wheel while the other spoke.

"You hear about that girl?" he asked.

Sabine slowed beside me.

I barely noticed.

"What girl?" the other man replied.

"The one from the church town two counties east. Ran off a few weeks back."

Something inside my chest tightened.

I told myself not to listen.

But the words kept coming.

"Pastor's family was involved somehow," the first man continued. "Or the pastor's niece. Something like that."

Sabine's hand brushed lightly against my wrist.

A silent warning.

Too late.

"They said the girl had… tendencies."

The word twisted in the air like something rotten.

"Troubled," the man added. "That's how her mother described her. Said she'd been battling sinful thoughts for months."

My stomach dropped.

The world seemed to tilt slightly beneath my feet.

"She tried to send the girl to one of those reform homes," the other man said. "A place run by the church. Said it might straighten her out."

Sabine's fingers tightened slightly around the crate she was carrying.

"But the girl ran before the men arrived."

The first man shook his head slowly.

"Shameful business. Her mother told the whole congregation the Devil had been whispering in her ear for years."

I couldn't breathe.

"Poor woman," the second man muttered.

"She did everything she could."

Sabine set the crate down.

The sound of glass bottles clinking together seemed to echo far too loudly.

"Let's go," she said quietly.

But the men weren't finished.

"They say the girl disappeared into the woods that night," the first man continued. "No one's seen her since."

He shrugged.

"Probably froze to death out there."

The other man nodded.

"Or worse."

A laugh.

Casual.

Indifferent.

"Either way," he said, "the town's better off."

Sabine grabbed my hand.

Not roughly.

Just firmly enough that I couldn't stay where I was.

She pulled me away from the wagon before the men could notice us standing there.

We walked in silence across the lantern-lit grounds.

The sounds of the circus returned slowly—the crackle of fire barrels, the distant rumble of wagons being unloaded, the faint music drifting from the musicians' tent.

But everything felt different now.

The world outside the circus had already buried me.

"Evelyn."

Sabine's voice was gentle.

I hadn't realized we had stopped walking.

The edge of the field stretched out behind us, the trees dark against the fading light of the sky.

"They believe her," I said quietly.

Sabine didn't answer right away.

"She told them I was wicked," I continued. "That I was… broken."

The words tasted bitter in my mouth.

"She told them God wanted me fixed."

The lantern light flickered across Sabine's face as she studied me.

"People believe the story that hurts them the least," she said softly.

"That one hurt her the least."

I stared out toward the dark trees beyond the field.

Somewhere in those woods was the road I had taken when I ran.

Somewhere behind that road was the house where my mother still knelt beside her bed every night and prayed for God to cleanse the world of things like me.

The town believed her.

The church believed her.

The world had already decided who I was.

Sabine stepped closer.

Her hand brushed lightly against mine.

"They don't know you," she said.

Her voice was steady.

"They never did."

I swallowed hard.

"And now they never will."

The lanterns across the circus grounds flickered brighter as night settled over the field.

Music rose from the main tent.

Laughter followed.

Life moved forward.

Something inside my chest loosened slightly.

The town might believe the story my mother told.

But the circus had never asked for that story.

Here, no one cared who I used to be.

Here, I was simply Evelyn.

And that felt like the beginning of something new.

Chapter Twenty

Under the Big Top

Lust and Shadows

Lilith found me just outside the Big Tent, where the last echoes of applause were still drifting through the night air. Lanterns swayed gently above the entrance, their golden light stretching long shadows across the sawdust path. My mind was still spinning from what I had heard those men saying about me. I must have looked unsteady, because Lilith tilted her head the moment she saw me, studying my face as if she could read every memory still echoing behind my eyes.

"Too many stories for one night?" she asked softly. Her voice carried that familiar velvet warmth, something teasing and knowing at the same time. She reached up and brushed a loose strand of hair away from my cheek, her fingertips lingering just long enough to make the skin there warm. "Or not enough?"

I opened my mouth to answer, but the words refused to form. My thoughts were racing too quickly, tangled somewhere between exhaustion and exhilaration. Everything about this place felt alive in a way the world I had come from never had. Every story I touched seemed to wake something deeper inside me—something that had been buried for years.

Lilith seemed to notice.

Her hand slid down to my wrist, her fingers closing lightly around it. "Come," she said, her voice dropping into something quieter, almost conspiratorial. "The show's finished. The real magic always happens after the lights go out."

She led me away from the lantern glow and the scattered performers lingering near the tent. The circus grounds stretched out beneath the moon, quiet now except for the distant creak of ropes and the soft murmur of voices drifting from other tents. We passed sleeping wagons and stacks of crates, the air thick with the scent of burnt sugar, sawdust, and fading firelight.

Lilith's tent waited at the edge of the performers' row, its dark canvas shimmering faintly in the moonlight. Something about it felt different from the others, as though the space inside held its own quiet gravity. When she pushed the flap aside and stepped in, the air changed instantly, warm and heavy with incense.

Velvet drapes hung along the walls, catching the golden glow of a single lamp burning on a small table. Shadows pooled in the corners of the tent, soft and deep, turning the space into something half hidden and intimate. The faint scent of wine lingered in the air, mixed with something darker that I couldn't quite place.

Lilith turned toward me slowly, her eyes never leaving mine.

"You've seen a lot tonight," she murmured. "Memories, pain, truths people spend their whole lives trying to bury." She stepped closer as she spoke, the lamp behind her casting her silhouette in warm gold. "But there's one truth you've been avoiding since the moment you arrived."

My pulse thudded heavily in my chest.

Before I could ask what she meant, she lifted her hand and brushed her fingers lightly across my cheek. The touch was gentle, but it carried a quiet certainty that made it impossible to pull away.

"You're burning inside, Evelyn," she whispered. "And you've spent your whole life pretending you aren't."

The words landed somewhere deep in my chest.

For a moment neither of us moved. Then Lilith leaned forward and kissed me.

The kiss was nothing like the hesitant one I had shared with Sabine days earlier. Lilith kissed with confidence, with a slow and deliberate certainty that made my breath catch almost instantly. Her lips moved against mine as though she already understood the shape of my desire, as though she had been waiting for the moment I stopped pretending it didn't exist.

My hands found her shoulders without thinking.

Her fingers drifted along my waist, the warmth of her touch sending quiet sparks across my skin. When the fabric of my dress slipped from my shoulders, the cool air brushed against my skin and made me shiver. Lilith didn't rush the moment. She simply studied me, her gaze moving slowly across my face like she was memorizing something important.

"You're beautiful when you stop hiding," she said softly.

The words made my throat tighten. No one had ever said something like that to me without judgment hiding behind it. My entire life had been built around shrinking myself, around burying anything that might invite suspicion or anger.

But here, in the warm shadow of her tent, none of that seemed to matter.

Lilith guided me gently onto the chaise near the lamp, her movements careful and deliberate. The world outside the tent faded away, leaving only the warmth of the lamplight and the quiet rhythm of my breathing. Her lips brushed along my skin in slow, thoughtful kisses that made every nerve in my body wake beneath her touch.

"Let go," she murmured near my ear. "There's no shame here."

Something inside me finally did.

The tension I had carried for years unraveled all at once, leaving me breathless and trembling. My fingers tightened against her shoulders as sensation surged through me like fire racing through dry wood. For a moment the entire world seemed to dissolve into warmth and light.

Then I saw her.

Sabine stood just inside the entrance of the tent.

She hadn't made a sound when she stepped inside. The lamplight caught the edges of her dark hair, turning the strands into flickers of gold and shadow. Her expression was unreadable—part flame, part ash, something wounded hiding just beneath the surface.

Our eyes met.

The moment lasted only a heartbeat.

Then Sabine turned and walked back into the darkness outside the tent.

My breath caught sharply in my chest. "Sabine—"

The name barely left my lips before Lilith kissed me again, slower this time, her hand rising to cradle the back of my head. The kiss wasn't demanding now. It was grounding, steadying me as the moment shifted around us.

"She knows," Lilith said quietly when she pulled away, her thumb brushing lightly across my cheek.

I stared at the tent entrance, half expecting Sabine to return. But the darkness outside remained still and empty.

"In this place," Lilith continued softly, "everyone chooses eventually."

I lay there afterward, the lamplight flickering softly across the velvet walls while my heart slowly steadied. My body still hummed with the aftershock of everything that had happened, every nerve alive in a way I had never allowed before.

Something inside me had shifted.

Desire no longer felt like something dangerous.

It felt like something powerful.

And though the image of Sabine standing in the doorway lingered like a fresh burn beneath my skin, I knew one thing with absolute certainty.

Tonight, I had stopped pretending.

And once the truth breaks free—

There is no going back.

Chapter Twenty-One

Under the Big Top

Ashes Between Us

I found Sabine near the edge of the woods, just beyond the broken carousel where rusted horses slept in frozen, crooked poses. Their painted eyes stared out into the darkness as if they were still waiting for music that would never return. The night air was thick with the smell of pine and damp earth, and the distant glow of the circus lights flickered faintly through the trees.

Sabine sat on a fallen log with her back to me, shoulders slightly hunched, her fingers idly plucking at a blade of grass like she was trying to read something written in its veins. She didn't look up when I approached, though I knew she had heard me long before my footsteps reached the clearing.

"I didn't mean for it to happen," I said quietly.

The words felt small the moment they left my mouth. The night hummed with cicadas, their steady song filling the silence between us. A breeze stirred the trees overhead, sending a ripple of whispering leaves through the branches, but Sabine remained perfectly still.

I moved closer and sat beside her, leaving just enough space between us that our shoulders didn't quite touch. "With Lilith," I added after a moment, though we both knew what I meant.

Sabine let the blade of grass fall from her fingers before finally turning her head. The lamplight from the distant tents brushed faintly across her face, and for a moment I saw something fragile in her expression—like porcelain cracked but not yet broken.

"Did she hurt you?" she asked.

Her voice was calm, but there was a brittleness beneath it, like thin ice over deep water.

"No," I whispered. "She didn't hurt me."

Sabine watched me carefully.

"She made me feel like I wasn't broken."

Something in her posture tightened. Her shoulders stiffened slightly, and her gaze shifted away toward the dark line of the trees.

"So she fixed you," Sabine said quietly.

"No." I shook my head, my voice firmer now. "She didn't fix anything. But she didn't make me feel ashamed either."

That made Sabine look back at me.

I exhaled slowly, my fingers knotting together in my lap as old memories pushed their way to the surface. "My mother always knew," I continued. "About me. About the way I looked at girls. She watched everything. Every glance, every smile. She said she could see the devil in my eyes."

Sabine's jaw tightened slightly.

"She tried to pray it out of me," I said softly. "Tried to drown it out of me. Threaten it out of me. She called it filth. Called me filth."

Sabine flinched, just barely, but I saw it.

I looked down at the edge of my sleeve, twisting the fabric between my fingers. "I've kissed girls before," I admitted. "Behind the chapel, in dark corners where no one could see us. But it was always the same afterward. Fear. Guilt. The feeling that we'd done something unforgivable."

The wind shifted again, carrying the faint scent of sawdust and smoke from the circus grounds behind us.

"Here," I continued slowly, "that fear has started to melt away. And it's terrifying."

Sabine didn't answer right away. She stared ahead into the trees, her expression thoughtful and guarded at the same time.

"I didn't plan to be with Lilith," I said. "But when she touched me… something inside me opened. Not because she's a woman. Because she saw me. And for the first time in my life, I didn't feel like I had to hide."

Sabine's voice was quiet when she finally spoke.

"Do you love her?"

The question hung in the air between us.

"I don't know," I said honestly. I lifted my eyes to meet hers. "But I know I feel something for her. And for you."

Sabine's gaze shifted away again, her jaw tightening as if she was holding something back.

"I care about you, Sabine," I continued. "Not just because you were kind to me when I arrived here. Not just because of the way your eyes burn when you speak the truth. But because I've seen your story now. I've felt it."

The memory of the burning village flickered through my mind.

"I know what you lost," I said gently. "And even after all that pain, you still fight to protect people like me."

Sabine remained silent, but the tension in her shoulders softened slightly.

"Lilith said something to me afterward," I added. "She said, 'She knows. We all choose, eventually.'"

Sabine stirred at that.

Her fingers brushed the bark of the fallen log, tracing its rough surface slowly.

"What does that mean?" I asked.

She hesitated before answering, brushing a loose strand of hair behind her ear. "It means that once you truly accept this place—once you embrace what the circus is and what it offers—you don't just perform here anymore."

Her gaze lifted toward the distant glow of the tents.

"You become part of it."

I felt a chill move down my spine.

"The magic changes you," Sabine continued quietly. "Time stops treating you the way it treats everyone else. Years pass outside these grounds, but here... we remain."

I swallowed. "You mean immortality?"

Sabine shook her head slightly. "Not exactly. We can still die. We still bleed. But the circus becomes an anchor. It holds us in place while the world moves on."

"And if someone leaves?" I asked.

Sabine's expression darkened slightly. "Then time remembers them again. And when it does… it takes back everything it was owed."

My breath caught.

"You've already begun to change," she added gently. "The fire in your hands. The way the mirror tent responded to you. The circus is calling you."

The words settled heavily in my chest.

"And if I choose to stay?" I asked quietly.

Sabine turned to look at me then, really look, as though she were searching for something hidden deep beneath the surface.

"Then this becomes your home," she said softly. "Your sanctuary. Your responsibility. The circus will claim a piece of you the same way it has claimed the rest of us."

I nodded slowly.

"And if I choose you?" I asked.

Sabine swallowed, something fragile flickering across her expression—hope, maybe, or fear.

"Then I'll be here," she said. "If that's what you truly want. But it has to be your choice, Evelyn. Not something you run toward just because you're trying to escape something else."

I shifted slightly closer to her, just enough that our knees brushed.

"I'm not sure of anything yet," I admitted. "But I want to be brave enough to find out. Not just about the circus. About myself. About what it means to want something without feeling ashamed of it."

Sabine's eyes softened.

"You don't have to choose tonight," she said quietly.

"I know."

I looked down at our hands resting between us.

"But I wanted you to know that you matter to me. Not just because we were both reborn from fire. You matter because you see me. The real me. And you never looked away."

My voice softened.

"When everything else in my life was burning down around me... you were the one who reached for me."

For a long moment neither of us spoke.

Then Sabine reached out and took my hand.

Her fingers laced through mine, warm and steady.

We sat there together beneath the trees, two girls shaped by trauma and magic, the silence between us no longer heavy with fear but with something quieter and deeper.

Something unfinished.

The wind carried the distant scent of sawdust and smoke from the Big Top.

And somewhere beyond the trees, I could feel the circus waiting.

Sabine could feel it too.

I knew it by the way her fingers tightened gently around mine.

Chapter Twenty-Two

Under the Big Top

The Knife Twins

The Knife Twins didn't mingle like the others.

They never laughed at Thorne's dry jokes or lingered by the fire after a show. They didn't drink the wine or join the quiet music that drifted between tents late at night. When the circus relaxed into its softer hours, Cassia and Lucien disappeared into the shadows, practicing somewhere beyond the reach of laughter.

And if you wandered too close while they trained, something in the air changed.

It wasn't fear exactly. It was sharper than that—like the instant before a blade meets flesh. A silent tension that hummed just beneath the skin.

But tonight, something pulled me toward them.

I followed the faint rhythm of metal ringing through the darkness. Steel striking steel. The sound carried through the backstage corridors like a heartbeat, steady and hypnotic.

When I slipped behind the curtain, I found them beneath a single flickering lantern.

Cassia and Lucien moved together in perfect, terrifying synchrony. Their bodies turned and shifted with impossible precision, knives flashing in silver arcs through the dim light. The blades spun between their hands like extensions of their bones—no hesitation, no wasted motion.

It was violence made beautiful.

A dance built from trust sharp enough to kill.

Their eyes never left each other.

Something about them prickled beneath my skin like static electricity. They were beautiful in the way dangerous things often are—youth frozen in time, as if sixteen was the last age their bodies remembered. Their cheekbones were sharp, their limbs lean and quick. Their dark hair clung damply to their temples as though they had just stepped out of rain.

There was something ghostlike about them.

Untouchable.

I didn't realize how close I had drifted until Cassia's knife stopped midair.

Her gaze snapped to mine.

"You want to know," she said.

Her voice wasn't accusing. It was almost curious.

I didn't answer.

I didn't have to.

Cassia stepped toward me slowly, the blade still balanced in her hand. Lucien lowered his own knives but said nothing, watching with a stillness that felt heavier than silence.

Cassia took my hand.

Her palm was cool when she pressed the knife handle into it.

The world shattered.

I was inside a memory.

But it wasn't mine.

Cassia and Lucien were children.

Their wrists and ankles were shackled together with rusted cuffs, iron collars tight around their throats. Chains connected them like living restraints, forcing their bodies to move as one even when they wanted to pull apart.

They stood beneath gaslight torches in a traveling freak show called **The Devil's Collection**.

The tent smelled of sweat, smoke, and sour liquor. Sawdust clung to their bare feet. The audience pressed close to the stage, their faces glowing with eager cruelty.

Behind them stood a man with a twisted spine and eyes like wet stone.

Father Dreg.

He told the crowd the twins were born from a demon woman he had purified with holy fire. That he had rescued them from hell itself.

But the truth was uglier.

He had found them abandoned in the ruins of a burned church.

And he saw profit.

Their act was pain.

Every night Lucien stood in the center of the ring, blindfolded, trembling but trained not to move. Cassia circled him with knives in her hands, throwing blade after blade so close to his body that the metal hissed past his skin.

The audience held their breath.

One wrong step.

One shallow breath.

And there would be blood.

Sometimes the crowd demanded more.

When they did, Father Dreg gave it to them.

Stage combat became real.

Cassia's blade would slice Lucien's arm. Lucien would return the cut across her ribs. Their blood soaked the sawdust while the audience roared their approval.

Once—only once—Cassia hesitated.

The knife trembled in her hand.

Father Dreg dragged her by the hair in front of the crowd, screaming about disobedience and sin. Then he forced Lucien to take the blade himself and carve a line across her side while the audience clapped like they were watching theater.

They were beaten if they cried.

Starved if they spoke out of turn.

But they endured.

The only gentleness they allowed themselves lived in the moments before each show.

Lucien would press his hand lightly against the place on Cassia's ribs where broken bones had healed crooked. Cassia would lean close enough to whisper against his ear.

"I'm still here," she would murmur.

"With you. For you."

Then they stepped into the ring.

And survived.

Until the night they decided it would be the last.

They had been planning it for weeks.

A stolen bottle of kerosene. A trail soaked through the canvas walls of the backstage tent. A single match hidden beneath Lucien's tongue.

They waited until the gaslights burned bright and the crowd roared loud enough to swallow the sound of their breathing.

Lucien struck the match.

The flame bloomed small and fragile for one second before he dropped it into the waiting oil.

Fire rushed upward like it had been starving.

At first the audience thought it was part of the show.

The flames spread through the tent rafters, licking hungrily across ropes and canvas. Smoke rolled across the ceiling like storm clouds gathering inside the building.

Then the screams started.

Cassia and Lucien didn't run.

Not yet.

They walked slowly through the chaos, past the audience clawing for the exits, past the burning stage where their blood had soaked into the floor night after night.

They walked straight to Father Dreg's trailer.

Inside, he was scrambling through drawers and safes, stuffing money into sacks while the fire devoured the world outside.

Lucien slammed the door shut behind them.

Cassia bolted the lock.

Dreg screamed.

They didn't answer.

They didn't look back.

The fire took him whole.

When the flames finally forced them outside, the circus grounds were already collapsing into ash. Smoke choked the sky. Horses screamed in their stalls. The crowd scattered through the night like frightened insects.

Cassia collapsed once they reached the edge of the woods.

But Lucien pulled her back to her feet.

They had to keep moving.

The trees swallowed them.

And then they heard the voice.

It wasn't spoken aloud.

It was something magical—something that tugged gently at their bones like a string tied to their souls.

They followed it into a clearing.

Fireflies floated through the dark like drifting sparks.

Madame Thorne stood waiting in the center of the light.

Her eyes glowed softly as she looked at them.

"You were never meant to be caged," she told them quietly.

"You were meant to carve your own path."

Cassia and Lucien didn't hesitate.

They chose her.

And the circus chose them back.

The world snapped back around me.

I gasped and dropped the knife.

Cassia caught it midair without looking.

My hands trembled. My heart pounded so hard it hurt.

"You see now," she said calmly.

"You were children," I whispered.

Lucien stepped out of the shadows beside her, his expression perfectly blank.

"We were forged," he said.

His voice was quiet but absolute.

"Children burn. Blades don't."

Cassia stepped closer and brushed her fingers lightly across my cheek. The touch was unexpectedly gentle.

"We're not like the others, Evelyn," she said softly. "We're a story you can only read once."

Then she turned and walked away.

Lucien followed.

Their hands hung close together as they disappeared into the darkness—close enough that they could have touched.

But they didn't.

And as I stood there in the lantern glow, one realization settled heavily into my chest.

They weren't just survivors.

They were vengeance.

Carved into flesh.

Wrapped in beauty and shadow.

Forever sixteen.

Chapter Twenty-Three

Under the Big Top

The Choosing

I found Madame Thorne in her tent long after the last of the crowd had faded into the quiet hum of the circus night.

Most of the lanterns had been dimmed by then, their light reduced to a soft golden glow drifting between tents like tired fireflies. The performers had mostly disappeared into their wagons or into the darker corners of the grounds where laughter turned low and private. Somewhere far off, a violin murmured through the air in slow, wandering notes. The scent of sawdust, smoke, and caramelized sugar hung thick beneath the canvas roofs.

But Thorne's tent stood apart from the rest.

The air around it felt different—still, expectant, as though the circus itself were holding its breath.

Inside, the space was dim except for a single candle burning beside a wooden vanity. The furniture was sparse, but everything carried a sense of age and intention. Strange artifacts rested on shelves along the walls—old rings, cracked porcelain masks, silver coins worn smooth with time. The canvas ceiling above seemed impossibly high, shadows climbing its length like silent spectators.

Madame Thorne stood before the vanity.

The strangest thing about it was the absence of a mirror. The polished wood frame held only empty space where glass should have been, leaving nothing for her reflection to rest in. Yet she brushed her long black hair with slow patience, each stroke of the brush deliberate, as though she were coaxing memories from the strands themselves.

"You're almost ready," she said before I had spoken a word.

Her voice carried easily through the tent, warm and certain, like a truth that had been waiting long before I arrived.

"Am I?" I asked quietly.

Even to my own ears my voice sounded distant, like it belonged to someone who had already begun stepping out of her old life.

Thorne set the brush down gently and turned toward me.

The candlelight caught her eyes, and for a moment they seemed to glow too brightly, reflecting something older than the flicker of flame. It was the same look I had seen when she spoke of the circus—as if she were both its keeper and one of its creations.

"You've seen us," she said softly. "Not the illusions. Not the spectacle we show the crowds." Her gaze moved over me with a quiet, measuring warmth. "You've seen the truth beneath the velvet and smoke."

I nodded slowly.

Because I had.

Sabine's fire had burned itself into my memory—the grief and fury that still lived in her bones centuries later. The Moth Girl's wings still rustled somewhere in the corners of my thoughts, fragile and beautiful despite the pain that birthed them. The Painted Man's living ink had shown me how guilt could crawl beneath the skin and refuse to die. The Knife Twins' vengeance had cut through me like cold steel, sharp and merciless.

And Lilith…

Lilith's touch still lingered like heat along my spine.

Every one of them had shown me something. A truth. A wound. A kind of survival that the world outside the circus would never understand.

"You know what it means to belong now," Thorne said.

The word settled into my chest with surprising weight.

Belong.

Not endure. Not hide. Not survive.

Belong.

She crossed the tent slowly and opened a tall wardrobe standing against the canvas wall. The doors creaked softly, revealing rows of costumes hanging inside like sleeping spirits waiting for their moment to wake.

Her hand moved through them until she found one.

When she lifted it free, the candlelight caught the fabric first.

Deep plum silk flowed over her arms like liquid twilight, and silver embroidery curled across the garment in long delicate tendrils that resembled drifting smoke or the slow rise of flame. The threads shimmered faintly, each one catching the light differently so the patterns seemed to move even when the fabric remained still.

The costume looked alive.

My breath caught in my throat.

"This is…" I said slowly, my voice barely above a whisper. "This is the costume you showed me when I first arrived. The one waiting in my tent."

Thorne inclined her head.

"You saw it before you understood because the circus saw you first," she replied gently. "It recognized you long before you recognized yourself."

She stepped closer and placed the garment carefully in my arms.

The silk was warm against my skin.

Not the warmth of cloth sitting near a fire, but something deeper, something that pulsed faintly like a second heartbeat.

"No more hiding," she said quietly. "Once you wear this, the girl who ran into the woods will no longer exist."

I looked down at the costume resting in my hands.

It was beautiful.

And terrifying.

Because I understood what she meant.

Putting it on wasn't just about performing.

It was a choice.

A declaration.

"Will it hurt?" I asked.

Thorne's lips curved into the smallest hint of a smile.

"No," she said. "But you will feel it."

I stepped behind the folding screen and began to undress.

Each layer of clothing fell away quietly—my blouse, my corset, the petticoats that had once wrapped me in the modesty my mother demanded. The garments slipped from my fingers and landed soundlessly on the floor, one after another, like fragments of a life that no longer belonged to me.

I stood for a moment in the dim light, bare and trembling.

Then I lifted the costume.

The silk slid over my shoulders easily, settling against my skin with uncanny precision. It hugged my waist and hips as though it had been stitched with my body already in mind. The silver embroidery shimmered faintly, the patterns curling and shifting with every breath I took.

It didn't feel like clothing.

It felt like a claim.

When my fingers found the clasp at the back of my throat, they trembled.

I fastened it.

And the world changed.

The air inside the tent dropped several degrees in an instant.

A wind erupted from nowhere.

It tore through the space with sudden force, snapping the canvas walls and sending the artifacts along the shelves rattling softly in their places. The candle flame shuddered wildly before extinguishing completely, plunging the tent into darkness for one suspended heartbeat.

Then smoke appeared.

Thin tendrils at first.

They rose from the floor like mist creeping across a river, curling around my ankles before winding slowly upward along my legs and arms. The air shimmered with silver ribbons of vapor, each strand twisting and drifting as though drawn toward me.

Outside the tent, voices began to murmur.

Performers.

Workers.

The circus was waking.

Madame Thorne stepped forward through the swirling smoke, her eyes glowing faintly like embers in the dark.

In her hands she held a mask.

It was silver and plum like the costume, its surface shaped in curling patterns that resembled flames rising across a girl's face. The metal gleamed softly in the returning candlelight as the wick flared suddenly back to life.

"You are not Evelyn," she said gently.

The words carried the weight of ceremony.

"Not the girl who ran from a house of fear. Not the child who was told her heart was something shameful."

She placed the mask in my hands.

"You are something else now."

For a moment I simply held it there, feeling the quiet pulse of the circus around me. I could hear the distant creak of ropes above the big top, the rustle of fabric shifting in the wind, the low hum of magic woven into every tent and wagon across the grounds.

The circus was alive.

And it was waiting.

Slowly, I lifted the mask and pressed it against my face.

The moment it touched my skin, heat bloomed through my body.

Smoke erupted around me in a sudden spiral, rising in twisting currents that wrapped around my arms and shoulders like living ribbons. The candle flame roared higher without a hand touching it, casting wild shadows across the tent walls.

The canvas ceiling rippled.

Outside, the murmuring voices grew louder.

The circus knew.

Somewhere deep inside me, a whisper unfurled.

She is the girl in smoke.

Not a runaway.

Not a sinner.

Not a secret hidden in the dark.

Something stronger.

Something the world outside could never understand.

When the wind finally stilled, the silence that followed felt sacred.

Madame Thorne looked at me with a quiet pride that felt centuries old.

"The crowd is waiting," she said softly.

I straightened.

The fear that had followed me through the forest, through the circus gates, through every memory I had witnessed was gone.

In its place was something steadier.

Something fierce.

"I'm ready."

Chapter Twenty-Four

Under the Big Top

Initiation

The drums began low, almost too soft to notice at first.

A slow, steady pulse rolled through the tent like a second heartbeat beneath the earth. The rhythm vibrated through the wooden supports, through the sawdust ring, through the soles of my feet where I stood waiting behind the curtain.

Boom.

Boom.

Boom.

Ancient. Patient. Summoning.

I stood in the shadows of the wings, dressed in plum and silver. The silk of the costume clung to my body like a second skin, warm and alive against my shoulders and waist. Every movement sent the silver embroidery shimmering faintly, the threads catching stray sparks of lantern light drifting through the tent. The mask rested against my face so lightly it almost felt like breath instead of metal, its curling flame patterns framing the world in flickers of shadow and gold.

Beyond the curtain, the crowd hummed with restless anticipation. Hundreds of voices murmured together, rising and falling like distant waves. The scent of sweat, sugar, and oil lamps thickened the air, and every so often the audience let out a ripple of laughter or excitement that fluttered against the canvas ceiling.

But I wasn't afraid.

I should have been.

I had never rehearsed this act. No one had taught me choreography or drilled me in the way Sabine had learned to bend fire to her will. No one had shown me how to command the stage, how to move beneath the weight of so many watching eyes.

And yet something inside me knew.

My muscles hummed with quiet certainty. My breathing had fallen into rhythm with the drums. It felt less like stepping into a performance and more like remembering something my body had always known.

Like the circus had carved a place in its soul for me long before I arrived.

Madame Thorne's voice echoed faintly in my memory.

You were always meant to be more than what the world allowed you to be.

The drums grew louder.

Boom.

Boom.

Boom.

Then the curtain lifted.

The tent beyond had transformed.

Lanterns hung from the high netting above the ring like captured stars, their golden light spilling down across the sawdust floor in soft waves. Smoke drifted along the ground, curling gently around the edges of the stage like morning fog rolling across a river. The entire crowd seemed to inhale at once as the curtain rose, their voices falling away into stunned silence.

I stepped forward.

The moment my foot touched the ring, the world beyond it disappeared.

The crowd faded.

The noise faded.

All that remained was the rhythm of the drums and the slow heat building in my chest.

The first movement came without thought.

I lifted my hands.

Flame bloomed from my palms.

It did not erupt violently the way it had the first time I lost control. Instead it unfurled slowly, elegantly, like ribbons of molten gold winding upward through the air. The fire curled around my wrists and forearms, spiraling in gentle arcs that flickered across my skin without burning.

It felt like greeting an old friend.

A ripple of gasps spread through the audience.

The flames followed my breath, responding to every subtle shift in my body. When I turned, they followed. When my arms rose, they stretched upward like living silk pulled toward the sky. I spun slowly, the fire tracing glowing circles around me, weaving through my fingers and across my shoulders in delicate loops of light.

I wasn't dancing the way performers practiced their steps.

I was moving with instinct.

Every twist of my body fed the flames something new—my fear, my anger, my longing for something beyond the narrow world I had escaped. The fire devoured those pieces of me eagerly, turning them into brightness and motion.

The girl who had run through the forest alone was dissolving in the heat.

I felt it happen.

Layer by layer.

Ash by ash.

The flames grew stronger as I moved, weaving together into long golden strands that stretched through the air around me. They coiled across my waist, curled behind my shoulders, and spun outward into wide circles that lit the tent in flickering amber light.

At the edge of the ring, I caught movement.

Sabine and Lilith stood half hidden in the wings.

Sabine's eyes glowed like hot coals beneath the lantern light, her lips parted slightly as she watched me. The fire reflected in her gaze as if it recognized something kindred in her soul. Lilith leaned beside her with one shoulder against the curtain, her expression softer than I had ever seen it, the sharp edge of her usual smirk replaced with something like awe.

The way they looked at me felt like a hymn.

Something dark and velvet stirred in my chest.

I danced for them.

For Sabine's burning gaze.

For the memory of Lilith's hands tracing fire across my skin.

My body moved differently now—no longer cautious or restrained. My steps flowed with confidence, each movement slow and deliberate, like smoke drifting through warm air. The flames responded eagerly, spinning outward from my wrists in long twisting ribbons.

This was who I was.

The fire grew bolder.

Golden threads stretched outward toward the edge of the ring, creeping through the air like curious vines reaching for sunlight. They spiraled gently toward the audience, hovering just inches from the faces of those in the front rows. Gasps and whispers spread through the crowd as the glowing tendrils danced just out of reach.

A child leaned forward, eyes wide with wonder.

"She's beautiful," he whispered.

The flames recoiled instantly, curling back toward me like obedient creatures returning to their keeper.

The air around me pulsed.

Something shifted.

The fire behind me surged upward suddenly, twisting into a towering column that burst outward with breathtaking force.

And then—

Wings.

Massive wings of living flame unfurled from my back, their span stretching across the tent in blazing arcs of gold and crimson. Each feather burned like a separate tongue of fire, flickering and shifting as the wings opened wide.

I felt them.

Heavy.

Glorious.

Power surged through my spine as the flames lifted higher.

The ground slipped away beneath my feet.

I rose into the air.

The crowd exploded into shouts and applause as I floated above the ring, suspended by nothing but fire and fate. The wings carried me upward in slow, graceful motion, the heat of them roaring softly in my ears as they beat against the still air of the tent.

From above, I could see everything.

The wide circle of the ring glowing beneath me.

The rows of stunned faces turned upward in awe.

Sabine standing with her hand pressed against her chest.

Lilith watching with parted lips like someone witnessing a miracle.

But this was no longer a performance.

This was transformation.

The wings blazed brighter for one final moment before a sudden gust of wind tore through the tent. The current whipped through the ring, scattering smoke and sawdust like drifting stardust. Lantern flames flickered wildly, and the canvas walls rippled as though the entire structure had taken a deep breath.

The circus itself was answering.

The wind swirled around me once—tight and deliberate.

A seal.

A blessing.

Then the current faded.

The wings dissolved slowly into glowing embers that drifted away like falling stars. My body lowered gently back toward the ring, the fire retreating into faint curls of smoke around my wrists as my feet touched the earth once more.

For a moment there was only silence.

Then the tent erupted.

Applause thundered through the air like a storm.

But I barely heard it.

What I felt instead was something deeper settling into my bones— ancient and certain.

The circus had seen me.

And it had claimed me.

I turned toward the wings.

Sabine stepped forward first.

Her expression was unreadable at first, but the fire in her eyes said everything her voice didn't.

Lilith followed beside her, one eyebrow lifted, her smile curling into something approving and hungry all at once.

I smiled back.

Open.

Certain.

Because the truth was finally clear.

I had chosen.

I had chosen them.

I had chosen this life.

And there was no going back now.

Chapter Twenty-Five

Under the Big Top

Entwined

The applause still echoed in my bones.

Even after the crowd had begun to drift away and the lanterns dimmed beneath the high canvas ceiling, I could still feel the rhythm of it humming inside my chest. The fire I had called into the world moments before had quieted now, settling somewhere deeper within me, warm and steady like an ember that would never fully fade.

I had given everything.

And somehow, I felt fuller than I ever had before.

Backstage, the circus had fallen into that strange hush that comes after something extraordinary. Performers moved quietly through the shadows, gathering props and whispering to one another in low voices. The scent of smoke and oil lamps lingered in the air, mingling with the sweetness of spun sugar drifting in from the fairgrounds outside.

But my attention found only two figures waiting near the velvet drapes.

Sabine stood closest to the stage, her golden eyes soft yet stormy in the lantern light. Her expression was composed, but there was something fragile beneath it, something that looked almost like awe. Just behind her lounged Lilith, one shoulder against the curtain, her arms folded loosely as she watched me approach. That familiar half-smile curved at her lips—part mischief, part awe.

Neither of them spoke.

They didn't need to.

I stepped toward them, and the space between us seemed to shift, as if the air itself understood that something had changed. The energy that pulsed through the circus tonight flowed between us like a living current.

Lilith reached for my hand first.

Sabine took the other.

Without a word, they guided me away from the stage and deeper into the shadows of the grounds. The sounds of the departing crowd faded behind us as we slipped between the rows of tents, past lanterns swaying gently in the night breeze.

When we reached Lilith's tent, she pushed the flap aside and ushered us inside.

The space was warm and dimly lit, velvet drapes softening the edges of the lantern glow. Cushions and blankets were scattered across the floor like a nest built for quiet moments between storms. The scent of incense curled lazily through the air, sweet and calming.

Sabine was the first to touch me.

Her hand rose to my face, cupping my cheek as her thumb brushed away a faint streak of soot along my jaw. The gesture was gentle, almost worshipful, as though she were afraid the moment might dissolve if she moved too quickly.

"You were magnificent," she whispered.

Her voice trembled slightly around the edges.

"You moved like something born of the stars."

I leaned into her touch without thinking, warmth blooming beneath my skin.

"I was born here," I murmured softly. "With you."

Behind me, Lilith stepped closer.

Her arms slipped loosely around my waist, drawing me back against her as her chin brushed my shoulder. Her presence was grounding and warm, her breath feathering softly against my ear.

"You chose us," she said quietly.

Her voice carried none of its usual teasing edge now. Instead it sounded steady, certain.

"And we choose you," she added, her fingers tightening gently around mine. "Again and again."

For a moment none of us moved.

Then something in the air shifted, subtle and electric, like the moment just before lightning breaks across the sky.

Sabine's fingers slid to the ties at the back of my costume, loosening them carefully. The silk fell from my shoulders in slow folds of plum and silver, pooling softly at my feet. Lilith helped with quiet patience, her hands warm against my skin as she freed the last of the ribbons and embroidery.

Their eyes lingered on me, not with hunger alone but with something deeper—wonder, maybe, or recognition.

As though they were seeing me clearly for the first time.

They shed their own layers just as slowly, Sabine's dark hair falling loose around her shoulders as she unfastened her corset, Lilith's inked skin emerging beneath the soft lantern glow. The tattoos along her arms shifted faintly, restless but calm, like living shadows stirred by the warmth between us.

We came together naturally after that.

There was no urgency in it, no frantic edge of desire. Instead the three of us settled among the cushions like pieces of a constellation slowly finding their place in the sky. Sabine's lips brushed mine in a kiss that felt deep and steady as the ocean tide, while Lilith's laughter—soft and breathless—followed close behind, warm against my neck.

Their touches were gentle, curious, loving.

Hands traced the quiet map of shoulders and arms, the curve of a cheek, the line of a collarbone. Every moment stretched long and luminous, the kind of closeness that exists beyond words.

Then Lilith inhaled sharply.

The tattoos along her arms stirred.

Black vines unfurled beneath her skin, blooming slowly outward like ink flowers awakening after a long sleep. They curled along her shoulders and ribs before slipping outward into the air itself, delicate tendrils of shadow weaving toward Sabine and me.

One brushed lightly along Sabine's spine, drawing a quiet shiver from her.

Another curled gently around my wrist.

The vines wrapped around us—not tight or constricting, but soft and deliberate, as though they were weaving something invisible between our bodies.

Binding us.

"I've never seen them do this before," Lilith whispered, her voice hushed with disbelief.

Sabine watched the shifting ink with wide eyes.

"They know," she said softly. "They feel it."

I placed my hand over Lilith's heart.

Beneath my palm the ink stirred again, gathering and shaping itself into something new. Slowly, delicately, a new mark bloomed across her skin—a flower opening into three curved petals, each one reaching toward the others.

At its center flickered a tiny flame.

I reached for Sabine's hand.

Lilith clasped mine.

Our fingers wove together like roots beneath the earth, grounding us in something deeper than fear, older even than the circus itself.

We were no longer three separate lives shaped by pain.

We were something shared.

Something chosen.

We stayed like that for a long while, wrapped together beneath the velvet drapes as the lantern light softened around us. Quiet laughter slipped between us now and then, along with murmured words that didn't need to be remembered to matter.

It wasn't about desire alone.

It was about being seen.

About being known.

About finding, at last, a place where love did not have to hide.

When exhaustion finally pulled us toward sleep, Sabine rested beside me with her fingers tracing idle patterns along my collarbone. Lilith lay with her head against my stomach, the new tattoo on her chest glowing faintly in the lantern light.

"You're one of us now," Sabine murmured.

Lilith lifted her gaze and smiled softly.

"Forever," she said, "isn't long enough for what I feel for you both."

I closed my eyes, my arms wrapped around them as the quiet heartbeat of the circus settled around us once more.

The fear that had once ruled my life had vanished.

In its place remained only warmth.

Only fire.

Only love.

And the endless magic of the circus that had brought us together.

Chapter Twenty-Six

Under the Big Top

The Celebration

The air in Lilith's tent was warm and fragrant, thick with the soft mingling of ash, jasmine, and something honey-sweet that clung to our skin. The lantern hanging from the central beam cast a golden glow across the velvet drapes, turning the shadows soft and dreamlike. For a while the three of us remained exactly where we were—entwined on the cushions like a quiet constellation—my head resting against Sabine's chest while Lilith's fingers traced slow, absent-minded spirals along my back.

Neither of them spoke.

They didn't need to.

Sabine's heartbeat thrummed steadily beneath my ear, grounding and warm, while Lilith's breathing brushed gently against my shoulder like a lullaby whispered through the night. I felt safe in a way I had never known before—safe enough to simply exist, without fear that someone might tear the moment away.

I didn't want to move.

I didn't want the magic of this moment to end.

But the soft rustle of fabric near the entrance of the tent pulled me slowly back into the world beyond us. The silk curtain fluttered aside, stirred by a presence that carried its own quiet gravity.

Madame Thorne stepped inside.

She wore a gown the color of deep wine, the fabric catching the lantern light in shifting waves that resembled smoke drifting beneath starlight. Her dark hair had been gathered loosely at the nape of her neck, and her eyes shone with a brightness that felt almost maternal as they took in the scene before her.

For a single breathless moment I froze.

Part of me still expected reprimand. A lifetime of caution made it difficult to shake the instinct to hide.

But then Thorne smiled.

Not the quiet, knowing smile she often wore before a performance.

This one was brighter.

Proud.

"Oh, my darlings," she said warmly, her voice soft as velvet. "You've found each other, haven't you? Truly found each other."

Her gaze lingered briefly on Sabine, then on Lilith, before finally settling on me.

"And you," she continued, her expression softening further. "You were magnificent tonight, Evelyn. You burned brighter than I have seen in many years."

Lilith sat up first, reaching for a robe that draped across a nearby chair and wrapping it loosely around herself. Sabine shifted beneath me, brushing a strand of hair away from my face as I rose beside her. Despite the sudden movement, the warmth between us remained, quiet and unbroken.

Thorne crossed the tent and lifted her hand to my cheek, her palm warm against my skin.

"You chose us," she said gently. "And now you are truly one of us."

There was no doubt in her voice.

No hesitation.

Just certainty.

"Come," she added, her eyes sparkling faintly. "Get dressed. The family is waiting."

"Family?" I asked.

Her smile widened.

"The circus celebrates its own," she replied. "And tonight, my dear, we celebrate you."

When we stepped into the main tent again, I barely recognized it.

Only hours earlier the space had held fire and spectacle, the ring blazing with flame beneath the roar of the crowd. Now the energy had shifted entirely. The sawdust ring had been cleared away, replaced with long wooden tables draped in cloths of gold and midnight blue. Lanterns floated overhead like captive stars, glowing with soft shades of lilac and pale blue that bathed the entire tent in gentle light.

Music drifted through the air—something played on strings, slow and wandering, like a melody remembered from a dream.

Platters of food covered the tables: roasted meats glazed in honey and spice, bowls of jewel-colored fruit, breads dusted with sugar and herbs. The scent of it all made the tent feel warm and alive, like a feast prepared in honor of something sacred.

Every soul in the circus had gathered.

The Knife Twins stood near the far end of the tent, their usual severity softened by candlelight as they murmured quietly to one another. The Painted Man leaned against a support pole, a thin silver thread glimmering through the lines of one of his living tattoos. The Moth Girl fluttered nearby, her delicate wings shifting softly as she laughed beside a young acrobat who looked utterly enchanted by her.

Even the elephant had joined the celebration.

Her massive shape rested comfortably near the tent's edge, her violet-painted toes decorated with garlands of flowers while she accepted apples from a giggling group of performers.

As soon as we entered, the room erupted.

Applause filled the air once again, though this time it was warmer—more personal. Smiles and cheers rose from every corner of the tent as people lifted their cups and called out my name.

Someone pressed a goblet into my hand, the drink inside warm and spiced with cinnamon.

Across the room, the Painted Man lifted his own glass and grinned.

"To the girl of smoke!" he called.

"To Evelyn!" the rest of the circus echoed, their voices rising together like a spell.

Heat rushed to my cheeks, but I didn't shrink away from their attention. I stood there between Sabine and Lilith and let them see me fully.

All of me.

For the first time in my life, I wasn't afraid of being seen.

The night unfolded in laughter and music.

We ate and danced and moved through the crowd like drifting embers carried on the same warm current. Sabine spun me once beneath the lantern light, her laughter soft and rare, while Lilith stole a goblet from someone's hand and declared it the finest drink in three countries.

Later, when the music slowed and the tables were nearly empty, Madame Thorne returned to my side.

She rested her hand gently over mine.

"You were meant for this," she said quietly. "The fire, the stage, the family. And they were meant for you."

I followed her gaze across the tent.

Everywhere I looked there was life—laughter, conversation, quiet affection. The circus pulsed with warmth like a living heart, every soul within it connected by invisible threads of shared history and survival.

For so long I had believed I was alone in the world.

Now I understood the truth.

This place wasn't just a refuge for broken people.

It was something far greater.

A sanctuary.

A family.

A home.

Chapter Twenty-Seven

Under the Big Top

The Beast Tamer

After the feast faded and the laughter softened into distant murmurs, the circus slowly began to settle. Lanterns dimmed one by one as performers drifted toward their tents, their voices trailing away into the quiet of the night. The long wooden tables still held the remnants of celebration—crumbs scattered across golden cloth, half-empty goblets reflecting the glow of lanternlight, chairs pushed crookedly aside from where dancers had spun only hours earlier. At the center of the grounds, the great fire burned low, its flames rising and falling in slow breaths as if the circus itself were finally resting.

Most of the performers had gone to bed, their silhouettes disappearing into the soft shadows between tents. A few lingered near the dying fire, speaking quietly or simply watching the embers glow. Lilith leaned comfortably against my side, her arm draped loosely around my waist as though she had no intention of leaving anytime soon. Her warmth was steady and grounding, and the gentle rhythm of her breathing made the night feel calmer than it had in days. On my other side, Sabine traced slow circles against the inside of my wrist, her fingertips light but deliberate. It was a habit she had developed without saying anything about it—a quiet way of anchoring me whenever my thoughts began to race faster than the world around me.

Sleep felt far away.

The celebration still hummed inside my chest, too bright and alive to simply fade into dreams. I had danced in fire only hours before, had felt the circus itself respond to my choice, had heard the applause of the family I never believed I would have. Yet the more I learned about this place, the more I realized how many stories still lived in its shadows.

My gaze drifted beyond the circle of firelight until it settled on a figure sitting just outside its glow.

The Beast Tamer.

He always seemed to exist on the edge of things. Even during the celebration he had remained mostly silent, watching the others with the same calm patience he carried everywhere. He had the stillness of someone who had seen centuries pass and found no need to rush through another moment.

When he noticed me watching him, he did not look away.

Instead, he rose from the shadows and stepped forward until the firelight touched his face. The flames illuminated the pale lines of his weathered skin, the faint scars crossing his jaw and temple like old maps drawn by time itself. His features were difficult to place in any particular age. He looked neither young nor old, but something in between—like someone who had existed long enough that time had simply stopped trying to measure him.

"You want to know," he said.

It wasn't a question.

I nodded anyway.

Sabine's fingers stilled briefly against my wrist as the Beast Tamer lowered himself across from us, sitting cross-legged beside the fire.

For a moment he simply watched the flames shift and curl over the blackened wood. When he finally spoke, his voice was quiet but steady, carrying the weight of someone who had told this story very few times.

"I am one of the oldest here," he said. "My story begins before steam and iron, before cities swallowed the night with lanterns and engines. It begins when forests were thicker and roads were fewer, when villages survived by staying forgotten."

He paused, running a hand slowly across his jaw as though brushing away memories that had gathered there.

"My sister's name was Aelira," he continued. "She was my whole world."

The way he said her name made something tighten in my chest.

"We lived in a small village pressed against the edge of the forest," he said. "The kind of place travelers passed without noticing. And that was exactly how we liked it. She was the light of that place— always laughing, always singing while she worked. Even in winter, when the snow came down so heavy it buried the road, she found ways to make the day feel warm."

The fire crackled softly between us, sending sparks drifting upward into the dark.

"We believed we were safe there," he said quietly. "But safety is a fragile illusion."

His hands tightened slowly around his knees.

"They came with the road," he said. "Travelers. Mercenaries. Men who carried their cruelty like a badge of honor. They saw our village as nothing more than a place to take what they wanted before moving on."

His voice did not shake, but the weight beneath it was unmistakable.

"They took her."

The words hung in the air.

"A group of them," he continued. "Drunk on their own power. Drunk on the knowledge that no one in a forgotten village could stop them."

Sabine leaned slightly closer to me.

"She was gone three days," the Beast Tamer said.

The firelight flickered across his face, catching the hard shine in his eyes.

"I found her on the fourth."

He stared into the flames as if the memory still lived there.

"She didn't look human anymore," he said softly. "They broke her body. And what they didn't break, they hollowed out."

Lilith's arm tightened slightly around my waist.

"She died in my arms," he said. "Whispering my name."

Silence settled over the fire.

Not the comfortable quiet of the circus at rest, but something heavier—like grief lowering itself gently into the space between us.

"I buried what was left of her," he continued. "And something inside me cracked open."

He lifted his hands toward the firelight.

"At first I thought it was grief," he said.

The skin of his palms shimmered faintly, glowing with a subtle warmth like embers hidden beneath ash.

"But it wasn't grief."

His eyes lifted to meet mine.

"It was rage."

A faint pulse of light moved beneath his skin.

"That was when the gift began."

"Or the curse," he added.

My voice barely rose above a whisper. "What kind of gift?"

"I began to see people differently," he said. "Not their faces or the words they spoke. I saw what lived inside them—the things they buried beneath smiles and manners. Their cruelty. Their hunger. The rot they carried in silence."

The fire shifted as a log collapsed inward.

"And when the darkness inside someone grew heavier than the light," he continued, "I could show them what they truly were."

"How?" I asked.

He met my gaze calmly.

"I turned them into beasts."

Not metaphorical beasts.

Real ones.

"Claws," he said. "Teeth. Bones twisted into shapes that matched the violence in their hearts."

Sabine whispered beside me, "You punished them."

He nodded.

"For years I wandered," he said. "Across forests and battlefields. Across towns where men hurt each other in the name of kings and faith and pride. Everywhere I went, I left beasts behind me—creatures that had once been men."

The firelight danced in his eyes.

"Until Thorne found me."

Lilith tilted her head slightly. "You mean you heard her."

A faint smile touched his mouth.

"Yes," he said. "Her voice came to me like fate. Like a thread pulling me away from the edge of something darker than vengeance."

"What did she say?" I asked.

"She didn't ask me to stop," he replied.

Instead, he said, she had offered him a stage.

"A place where the beasts could exist not as hidden curses, but as something seen," he explained. "She told me if I was going to change them, they had to live with what they had become. Every night. Before an audience."

"Penance," Sabine murmured.

"Yes."

The Beast Tamer stared into the fire again.

"There is one among them now who was never meant for the stage," he said after a moment. "A man who slipped backstage after a show, disguised as a patron. He found the Human Marionette."

He didn't need to say more.

My stomach turned cold.

"Thorne knew," he said quietly. "She always does. The man screamed as the change took him—screamed until his voice became a howl. Now he performs in chains, covered in fur and rage, dancing at the edge of the ring."

"And you control them?" I asked.

He shook his head slowly.

"No," he said. "I guide them. They remember what they once were. And they remember the choices that made them this way."

He looked down at his glowing palms before lifting his gaze back to me.

"I did not become the Beast Tamer because I loved monsters," he said.

The fire reflected in his eyes like twin flames.

"I became him because the world refused to believe in justice."

Sabine squeezed my hand gently beside me. "We all become something else when we carry pain too long," she said softly.

The Beast Tamer nodded once.

"Here," she continued, "we simply wear it on the outside."

I looked at him again, seeing him differently now.

Not a monster.

Not a villain.

Just another soul the world had broken before the circus found him.

Another protector standing watch over a family built from the wreckage of other lives.

And as the fire crackled quietly beneath the open sky, I realized something else.

Every one of us had arrived at the circus through fire.

But here—

we had learned how to live with the flames.

Chapter Twenty-Eight

Under the Big Top

The Human Marionette

The fire crackled softly at the center of the circus grounds, its golden glow washing over the small circle of faces gathered around it. The night had grown quieter as the hours stretched on, the earlier laughter and music replaced with something more reflective. One by one the stories had unfolded—each heavier than the last, each revealing another scar hidden beneath the glittering illusion of the circus.

Yet no one turned away.

The fire seemed to hold us there, its slow-burning flames breathing warmth into the cool night air as though the circus itself wanted these truths spoken.

Then she stepped forward.

Silence fell over the circle with the quiet reverence of a held breath.

The Human Marionette.

She did not speak, as she never did. But something about her presence changed the air around her, as though the wind itself had paused to watch. The gauze layers of her pale skirts rustled softly as she moved into the firelight, the delicate fabric whispering like moth wings brushing against glass.

Her arms rested stiffly at her sides.

Above her, just barely visible in the shifting glow of flame, the faint shimmer of strings appeared. They trailed from her wrists and elbows, from her ankles and the base of her spine, glimmering like strands of silver caught in moonlight.

Music drifted up from somewhere unseen.

A violin.

Slow. Melancholic. The kind of melody that felt like it had lived inside sorrow long before it found sound.

She began to dance.

At first the movement was breathtaking in its grace. Her foot slid forward with the soft precision of a ballerina trained since childhood. She turned in a slow pirouette, skirts whispering around her legs, her toes brushing the earth so lightly it seemed she barely touched it at all.

For a moment, she looked like something delicate and whole.

Then the strings tightened.

Her body jerked slightly, the movement too sudden to belong to a dancer's will. Her arm lifted sharply, her head tilting at an angle that no living girl would choose for herself. The invisible threads guiding her trembled in the firelight, pulling her limbs into motion that was beautiful and terrible all at once.

She was no longer dancing freely.

She was being moved.

The fire shifted.

Its flames rose higher, sharpening and twisting as though a silent wind had stirred them. The orange glow curled and spiraled above the logs, forming shapes within the heat—images that unfolded like living memory.

Her story.

In the fire we saw a stage bathed in golden light.

She was there again, whole and radiant, dressed in pale silk and ribbons that glimmered beneath chandeliers. The applause surrounding her was thunderous, echoing across a grand theater filled with velvet seats and jeweled balconies. She moved across the stage with impossible lightness, every leap graceful, every turn flawless.

She was a prodigy.

The pride of the ballet.

Critics wrote poetry about her performances instead of reviews. Audiences traveled across cities just to witness the way she moved, as though gravity itself had forgotten how to touch her.

The fire flickered, shifting the vision again.

A royal court appeared, rich with velvet drapes and glittering jewels. Noblemen and ladies watched her with fascination, their whispers weaving through the air like silk threads. A letter sealed in gold was delivered into her trembling hands—an invitation to join a prestigious company that traveled the courts of kings and emperors.

A chance to leave.

A chance to become something greater than the daughter of a bitter man.

In the fire we saw her pack a small bag beneath the dim light of her bedroom. She folded her dance shoes carefully, as though they were sacred objects. Her heart beat with a fragile hope as she imagined the life waiting for her beyond the walls of that house.

But the fire darkened.

Her father found the bag.

His rage erupted like a storm breaking across the quiet room. His voice shook the walls as he screamed about betrayal and shame, about a daughter who belonged to him and no one else. In his eyes she was not a girl with dreams but a possession—a creation he believed he owned.

If he could not keep her, then no one would.

The flames trembled.

We saw him standing beside her bed while she slept, the hammer heavy in his hand.

The first strike was quiet.

The second was not.

The fire flashed violently as the vision showed the terrible truth. Bone shattered beneath the blow. Her knees—her beautiful, irreplaceable dancer's knees—were destroyed with brutal precision.

Her screams filled the vision though no sound left the woman standing before us.

The fire revealed her crawling across blood-slick floorboards the next morning, clutching her ballet shoes like lifelines while agony tore through her body. Her future had been stolen in a single night, her dreams crushed beneath the weight of a man who believed love meant ownership.

But the flames did not fade.

They shifted again.

At the window of that broken room appeared a figure woven from shadow and smoke.

Madame Thorne.

She stood there quietly, her eyes filled not with pity but with something deeper—understanding .

She held out a hand.

The broken girl took it.

And the strings appeared.

They flowed from Thorne's fingers like silver threads spun from moonlight, curling gently around shattered limbs and broken bones. The magic moved slowly, carefully, weaving through her body as though stitching porcelain back together after it had been dropped.

The threads lifted her.

Not to walk.

But to dance.

She would never be the girl she had once been.

But she would move again.

Back beside the fire, the Marionette's dance grew faster. Her body twisted and turned with heartbreaking precision, the strings guiding her limbs into movements that were both graceful and tragic. Each spin felt like a memory of what she had lost, each bow a farewell to the life that had been taken from her.

The violin rose into a final aching note.

When she stopped, she stood facing all of us.

Her chest rose slowly, as though each breath had become something sacred.

She did not smile.

But she bowed.

The movement was slow and deliberate, a performer's final acknowledgment of the audience watching her story unfold.

Then she turned.

The gauze of her skirts drifted softly behind her as she stepped away from the firelight and disappeared into the darkness beyond the tents. The faint shimmer of her strings faded with her, dissolving into the night as the violin's last note fell silent.

For several moments, no one spoke.

The fire popped quietly as another log shifted inward.

I exhaled only when Sabine's fingers closed gently around my hand.

"She dances like it's all she has left," I whispered.

Lilith's voice was softer than usual when she answered.

"Because it is."

Somewhere beyond the canvas walls of the tent, hidden in the dark where the performers' paths wound between lanterns and shadows, we heard the faint creak of strings retreating into silence.

And the fire burned on.

Chapter Twenty-Nine

Under the Big Top

Her

The fire was dying behind us, its once-roaring flames now reduced to a slow halo of embers glowing softly in the dirt. The warmth still reached our backs as we stepped away, but the bright energy of the celebration had already begun to fade into something quieter. Laughter still carried from the dinner circle in small bursts— someone retelling a joke, someone else clinking a glass—but it felt distant now, like echoes from another world.

The magic of the night had shifted.

The circus was settling into one of its deeper moods, the kind that lived beneath the performances and lanternlight, where truths seemed to gather more easily.

I needed air.

Or maybe I just needed them.

I slipped quietly from the edge of the campfire circle, brushing sawdust from my skirt as I stepped beyond the reach of the lanterns. I hadn't gone more than a few paces before Sabine rose from her place beside the fire and followed without a word. Lilith came next, moving with the same effortless silence she carried everywhere, her shadow stretching long across the moonlit grass.

None of us spoke.

We didn't need to.

The three of us walked beyond the last row of tents, past the wagons painted in fading colors and the quiet shapes of sleeping animals. The night air grew cooler as the circus lights faded behind us, replaced by the soft hush of the woods that bordered the clearing.

Tall grass brushed against our legs as we stepped into the meadow beyond the camp.

Wildflowers swayed gently in the night breeze, their pale petals glowing faintly beneath the moon. The sky stretched wide above us, heavy with stars, the moon hanging low and bright as if it had come closer just to watch.

We found a place near a fallen log at the edge of the trees.

Sabine sat first, leaning back against the rough wood before gently pulling me down between her legs. Her arms wrapped around my waist in an instinctive motion, strong and protective without ever feeling possessive. I leaned back against her chest, letting the quiet steadiness of her presence settle the restless energy still humming inside me.

Lilith lowered herself beside us, close enough that her shoulder brushed mine. She leaned forward and pressed a soft kiss to my shoulder, her lips warm against my skin.

It felt like a greeting.

A promise.

We're here.

We see you.

For a moment, none of us spoke. The night hummed softly around us—the distant chirp of insects, the rustle of leaves shifting in the trees, the faint murmur of voices drifting from the circus behind us.

I didn't want to break the peace of it.

But the words had already begun to burn inside my chest.

"My mom used to say I was like *her*," I murmured finally, my voice quieter than I expected. I hadn't even meant to say it out loud. The confession slipped out of me like breath. "She'd spit it like poison every time I slipped up. Or talked back. Or cried."

Sabine's arms tightened slightly around my waist.

Lilith grew still beside me.

"'You're just like her,'" I continued, staring out into the tall grass as the memory surfaced. "She said it like it was the worst thing I could possibly be."

The words tasted strange in the open air.

"I don't even know who she meant," I admitted softly. "She never said. Just… *her.* Like some ghost I was supposed to be afraid of becoming."

The stillness around me changed.

It was subtle—so subtle that anyone else might have missed it.

But I felt it immediately.

Sabine's arms went rigid for a heartbeat before she forced them to relax again. Lilith's breath caught quietly beside me, the sound barely more than a whisper against the wind.

Something in the air shifted.

Like pressure before a storm.

"I always thought it was just another way to make me feel small," I added quietly. "Another way to remind me I was wrong somehow."

No one answered right away.

The silence stretched long enough that I almost regretted bringing it up at all.

Then Lilith spoke.

Her voice was barely louder than the wind moving through the grass.

"We do."

I turned toward her, confusion flashing through me.

"What?"

Lilith's eyes met mine in the moonlight.

"We know who your mother meant."

The world tilted.

For a moment, I forgot how to breathe.

"What are you talking about?" I asked, the words tumbling out faster now. "How could you possibly know—?"

Sabine still hadn't looked at me.

Her gaze was fixed somewhere beyond the trees, her jaw set in a tight line.

"You… what do you mean you know?" I pressed.

Sabine finally spoke, though her voice was low and careful.

"It's not our story to tell."

The answer landed like a stone dropped into still water.

I stared at her, then at Lilith, trying to understand what I was seeing in their faces.

It wasn't fear.

But it wasn't surprise either.

"How long have you known?" I asked quietly.

Neither of them answered right away.

Lilith reached out slowly and took my hand in hers.

"We have always known of you and your story, you've earned the truth, Evelyn," she said gently. "But that part of your story belongs to Thorne. She's the one who has to tell it."

The air around us felt heavier now, filled with invisible threads pulling everything closer together.

I suddenly understood something I hadn't before.

I wasn't just part of the circus.

I was connected to it somehow.

Stitched into its history in ways I didn't yet understand.

My throat tightened as old memories crept back to the surface.

"She always made me feel like I was broken," I said quietly. "My mom. Every time I looked at a girl too long, every time I felt something real, she acted like I was turning into something horrible."

Sabine's arms tightened again, this time more gently.

"Like I was slipping closer to being unfixable," I continued. "Like there was something inside me she couldn't stand to look at."

Lilith squeezed my hand.

"Or someone she was afraid of," she said softly.

Sabine finally lowered her head, pressing her lips gently to my temple.

"Or someone she hated," she added.

I nodded slowly, letting the truth settle inside me.

"But being here…" I whispered. "Being with you both… it feels like I'm remembering something."

The night breeze stirred the grass around us.

"Like I'm remembering who I was before she made me ashamed of it."

Sabine's arms wrapped more securely around my waist as she leaned forward, her lips brushing my temple again.

"You're not broken," she said.

Lilith lifted my hand to her chest, pressing it against the steady rhythm of her heart.

"You were never broken," she echoed.

Their warmth surrounded me like a shield against every voice that had ever tried to convince me otherwise.

And for the first time, the pieces of myself didn't feel scattered anymore.

I wasn't the girl running away from something.

I was the girl becoming something.

And somewhere inside the circus, waiting behind secrets and stories older than I could imagine, was the truth about *her.*

Soon, I would have my answers.

Chapter Thirty

Under the Big Top

The Curse and the Blood

It was Sabine who took my hand this time, her fingers threading through mine with quiet certainty as she guided me through the silver-washed dark of the circus grounds. Lilith walked beside us, unusually silent, her usual confidence softened into something more watchful. The lanterns behind us swayed gently in the wind, casting long ribbons of light across the painted wagons and sleeping tents. Somewhere in the distance an animal shifted in its stall, the faint clink of metal echoing through the night air. None of us spoke as we crossed the quiet grounds, but the silence didn't feel empty. It felt heavy with anticipation, like the moment before a storm finally breaks.

The path toward Madame Thorne's tent seemed longer than usual. My chest felt tight with a strange gravity, a coiling certainty that the truth I had been circling was finally within reach. I could feel it the way you feel lightning before it splits the sky—an electric knowing that something inside my world was about to crack open.

When we reached the tent, the entrance flap was already unlatched.

Warm light spilled across the grass in a soft golden glow, flickering with the restless movement of candle flames. The moment we stepped inside, the air changed. It felt thicker here, older somehow, as if time itself moved differently within the walls of this place. The scent of smoke and something faintly herbal lingered in the air, wrapping around me like the memory of a fire that had never truly gone out.

Madame Thorne sat at a wooden table near the center of the tent. A single candle burned beside her, its flame stretching tall and steady as though even the fire recognized her authority. Her hands were wrapped around a goblet filled with liquid so dark it was nearly black. She lifted her eyes before we had fully stepped inside.

"Close the flap," she said quietly. "We have much to speak of."

Sabine hesitated for only a moment before stepping back. Lilith brushed my arm as she passed me, her fingers lingering there for a brief second—a warning and a promise in the same breath. They exchanged a quick glance between them before slipping outside into the night. The tent flap fell closed behind them with a soft rustle of canvas.

Suddenly I was alone with Thorne.

"You knew I'd come," I said, my voice quieter than I expected.

She inclined her head slightly, studying me with the calm patience she seemed to carry through centuries. "I have always known," she said. "Long before you were born."

The certainty in her voice made something tighten in my chest. I stepped closer to the table, the candlelight flickering across the worn wood between us.

"They told me you know who she is," I said. "The 'her' my mother always compared me to."

For a moment Thorne simply watched me. There was no surprise in her expression, no confusion. She didn't ask me to explain. She didn't need to. She already understood exactly what I had come for.

Slowly she rose from her chair, lifting the goblet in her hand. The liquid inside caught the candlelight strangely, its surface shifting with colors that did not belong to wine.

"Drink," she said.

The word hung in the air between us.

I hesitated, then reached for the goblet. The stem felt heavier than it should have in my hand, as though the glass itself carried history within its weight. When I lifted it to my lips, the scent rising from it was unfamiliar—smoke and spice and something wild and ancient.

The liquid was thick when it touched my tongue. Hot. It tasted like fire melting into blood.

And then the world disappeared.

The floor dropped out from beneath me as though gravity itself had loosened its hold. The tent dissolved into light, the candle flame stretching into a blazing column before everything shattered into something else entirely.

Suddenly I was not myself anymore.

I was her.

The world unfolded through different eyes, brighter and sharper than anything I had ever known. I was a child running barefoot through wide green meadows, the tall grass bending beneath the wind in shimmering waves. Flowers bloomed wherever I passed, their colors bright and fragile. But moments later those same petals wilted, fading as the strange magic pulsing through my small body brushed against them.

I didn't understand it yet.

My parents did.

At night I heard them whispering behind the thin walls of our cottage. Fear threaded through their voices like thorns through ivy. They called me their miracle, but the word trembled every time they spoke it. Miracles were blessings. But miracles were also dangerous.

One afternoon a rider arrived in the village.

His cloak carried the colors of the king.

Gold was offered. Land. Titles. Promises of protection.

My parents accepted.

They traded me away like livestock.

I was eight years old.

The castle was colder than any place I had ever known. The stone walls swallowed sound and warmth alike, leaving the halls filled with an echoing chill that seeped into my bones. By day I scrubbed floors until my fingers cracked from harsh soap and cold water. By night I carried trays of wine through corridors filled with laughter that did not belong to me. The nobles barely noticed the small servant girl moving quietly among them.

Until the night the king passed me in the corridor.

Our eyes met.

And the words slipped from my mouth before I even understood them.

"You will die in your sleep within the month."

The hall fell silent.

The king did not die.

But his brother did.

From that moment forward I was no longer a servant.

I was something useful.

The king married me when I turned twelve. He told the court it was an act of protection, a kindness meant to shield a young girl from cruel gossip. But I understood the truth. He wanted my magic. My visions. He wanted a bloodline touched by prophecy.

And he got one.

When I felt the first flutter of life inside me, hope bloomed despite the fear. I prayed the child would not inherit the darkness that surrounded her father. I prayed she might live freely in a world untouched by crowns and curses. But the king saw something entirely different. He saw conquest. A seer born to a seer. A bloodline he believed could bend the future itself.

I knew then that I had to run.

I planned my escape carefully, gathering courage in secret while pretending obedience before the court. When the night finally came, I fled with the child hidden beneath my cloak.

But the king discovered my plans.

Before they captured me, I found a glade deep within the forest where ancient trees stretched toward the sky like silent guardians. There, beneath their shadow, I placed my baby upon the moss and whispered a spell over her. Time would not touch her. Not until I returned.

Then they dragged me back in chains.

The execution came quickly. They bound me to the stake in the center of the courtyard as the villagers gathered to watch. When the torches touched the wood, the flames climbed higher and higher around me.

But I did not scream from pain.

I screamed from rage.

Something inside me shattered open as the fire rose. My magic surged upward, answering the flames rather than fearing them. The fire did not consume me. It became me. The curse wrapped itself around my bones, burning its way into every part of my being until immortality itself was forged within the blaze.

When the flames died, the kingdom fell with them.

And when the ashes cooled, I returned to the forest.

The child waited exactly where I had left her.

Untouched by time.

Perfect.

But I knew I could not give her the life I now carried.

So I waited.

I built something instead.

A sanctuary.

A place for the broken and the cursed and the abandoned souls the world refused to understand.

I built the circus.

Centuries passed.

Then one day a woman came to me. She was hollow with grief, haunted by the life she could never create. She begged for a child with a desperation that shook even my ancient heart.

And I gave her mine.

The vision shattered.

I collapsed onto the floor of Thorne's tent, gasping as air rushed back into my lungs. The wooden boards beneath my hands felt painfully real after the storm of memory that had just torn through me.

Madame Thorne knelt before me.

"You saw," she said quietly.

"It was real," I whispered.

My thoughts raced as pieces of my past fell into place with terrifying clarity. The drawings in my journals. The strange stories that had poured from me since childhood—women with wings, storms born from screams, flames that blossomed instead of burning.

"It was all real," I said, my voice shaking. "The things I saw. The things I wrote… they were visions."

Thorne's expression softened, something ancient and aching flickering behind her eyes. "They were echoes," she said. "Threads of the magic that lives inside you. You were born carrying my power, Evelyn. It has been speaking to you your entire life."

"You are my child," she continued gently. "Born of fire. Hidden in silence so the world would not destroy you before you were ready."

"My mother always said I was like her," I murmured.

Thorne nodded slowly. "She knew enough to be afraid."

The fire inside my chest flickered to life again, stronger now.

"What am I?" I asked.

For the first time, Thorne smiled—not with happiness, but with quiet awe.

"You are a beginning," she said softly. "The child of prophecy and flame. You are my legacy."

Outside the tent, the wind began to howl across the circus grounds, rattling the canvas walls like an old friend returning home.

"And now," she said, her voice dropping to a whisper, "you must choose. You may remain the girl you were… or you may become what you were always meant to be."

Inside me, the past unraveled and rewove itself into something vast and sacred all at once. I was no longer only the girl who had run from a cruel home or the frightened child who filled journals with dreams she didn't understand. Fire and blood and prophecy lived inside me now, pulsing through my veins like a second heartbeat.

I understood that my story had never truly belonged to me alone.

I lifted my head and met her gaze.

I was ready.

Chapter Thirty-One

The House Without Her

The door slammed harder than it needed to, rattling the thin glass in the hallway frame.

"Evelyn?" her father's voice echoed through the house, hopeful despite the exhaustion lacing it. His boots struck the hardwood floor in steady steps as he crossed the living room, already loosening the stiff collar of his work shirt. "Sweetheart? I'm back early tonight—where are you?"

Silence answered him.

He paused in the middle of the room, frowning slightly as he glanced around. Everything was neat—too neat. The furniture sat exactly where it always had, the cushions smoothed flat, the small decorative Bible centered perfectly on the coffee table. The lamps had been dimmed low, leaving the corners of the room shadowed and cold. There were no signs of life. No music drifting from Evelyn's room, no soft hum of her voice, no scattered notebooks or sketches left behind.

The house felt wrong.

"Carolyn?" he called.

His wife stepped out from the hallway with her arms folded tightly across her chest. The sharp line of her posture told him immediately that something was wrong. He knew that look well. It was the look she wore when judgment had already been passed.

"Where's Evelyn?" he asked.

"Gone," Carolyn replied flatly.

He blinked, the word taking a moment to settle into meaning. "Gone where?"

"She ran away."

For a moment he thought he must have misheard her.

"Ran away?" he repeated slowly. "What the hell do you mean she ran away? When? Why didn't you write me? Send a wire? Something?"

Carolyn didn't move. Her face remained stiff, her expression cold and unmoved.

"Because I don't care that she's gone," she said sharply. "That's one less sinner I need to try and save."

The words hit him like a slap.

He stared at her, trying to make sense of what she had just said. "Wait… what do you mean *save*? What happened while I was gone?"

Carolyn stepped closer, her eyes gleaming with something bitter and triumphant.

"I had her locked in the cellar, John," she said. "She was going to be taken to St. Vincent's Restoration Home for Girls. A place for healing. A place where they could cleanse her soul and set her right. Everything had already been arranged."

John felt the floor shift beneath him.

"You… locked her in the cellar?" he asked, his voice suddenly thin.

"She was waiting to be taken in the morning," Carolyn continued, her voice hard with conviction. "But she ran. Just like her. That godless little creature she is."

His stomach dropped.

The air rushed out of his lungs as if someone had punched him square in the chest.

"You imprisoned our daughter?" he demanded, his voice rising. "What the hell is wrong with you?"

Carolyn's nostrils flared.

"She's not ours, John!" she shouted.

The room seemed to freeze.

"What did you just say?" he asked quietly.

Her eyes burned with something that had clearly been waiting years to surface.

"I was barren," she snapped. "God punished me for the sins of my youth. I couldn't conceive. No matter how many prayers I said, no matter how many nights I begged Him for mercy."

She laughed once, but there was no humor in it.

"But then she came."

John's hands began to shake.

"What do you mean she came?"

"A woman brought her," Carolyn said. "A strange woman. Cloaked. I don't even remember seeing her face clearly. I had prayed for a sign, prayed for a child, and then suddenly Evelyn appeared in our lives as if she had been sent by heaven itself."

Her mouth twisted bitterly.

"But she wasn't a miracle, John. She was unnatural."

He stared at her in disbelief.

"You're telling me that all these years… you lied to me?"

"I tried to raise her right!" Carolyn shouted. "I tried to save her soul. But she was never normal. Always dreaming. Always drawing strange things in those journals of hers. Women with wings. Storms she claimed she could scream into existence. Fire that grew like flowers."

Her voice dropped into a furious whisper.

"And the girls."

John closed his eyes briefly.

"I tried to strip the sin out of her," Carolyn continued. "I tried to break it before it took root. But I couldn't. She was already lost. She always was."

The room tilted around him.

Carolyn stepped closer, her voice dripping with hatred. "She's gone back to them. To that circus. To her. That devil woman who poisoned her mind. She's returned to where she truly belongs."

John looked at his wife as if he were seeing her for the first time.

"She told me," he said quietly. "She tried to tell me what was happening here. I thought she was exaggerating. Being dramatic. I thought maybe she misunderstood you."

His voice cracked slightly.

"But she wasn't lying."

Carolyn lifted her chin defiantly. "I saved her. Or at least I tried to."

"You destroyed her," he said.

The truth of it settled heavily in his chest.

"And I let you."

Without another word, he turned and grabbed his coat from the hook beside the door.

Carolyn's voice rang out behind him, shrill with righteous fury.

"If you go after her, you turn your back on everything God wanted for this family!"

John paused at the door.

For a moment he considered the life behind him—the house, the marriage, the quiet routine he had spent years believing was normal.

Then he opened the door.

"No," he said quietly.

"I turn my back on you."

The door slammed behind him.

***

The carriage wheels rattled violently over the uneven road as he pushed the horses faster into the night. Fog curled low over the countryside, swallowing the narrow path ahead of him. The lantern hanging from the side of the carriage swayed wildly with each bump, its golden light swinging across the road in frantic arcs.

His heart pounded against his ribs.

He didn't know exactly where he was going.

But something was pulling him forward.

The night Evelyn disappeared, something inside him had snapped. He had been working late at the rail office, hunched over freight ledgers and signal schedules, when the feeling hit him suddenly—a deep, aching pressure behind his ribs that made him grip the edge of his desk.

At first he thought it was a heart attack.

A cold wind had howled down the tracks at that exact moment, rattling the windows and shaking the signal posts outside. He remembered gasping for breath, waiting for the pain to worsen.

But it hadn't been pain.

It had been knowing.

Now, as the carriage raced through fog and darkness, he finally understood.

Evelyn hadn't just run away.

She had stepped into something larger than the life she had been trapped in.

The house he had left behind had never truly been a home. It had been a cage, built carefully and quietly around a girl who had never belonged inside its walls.

And Evelyn—his daughter, his strange, brilliant girl with storms hidden behind her quiet eyes—had finally broken free.

He tightened the reins in his hands.

He would find her.

He didn't care if devils or angels had claimed her.

She was his daughter.

And he would not lose her again.

Chapter Thirty-Two

Under the Big Top

The Girl Who Was Chosen

The tent flap still whispered when it moved, even hours after I left Madame Thorne's side.

The sound followed me as I walked through the quiet heart of the circus, soft canvas brushing against wooden poles, lanterns flickering low in the night wind. I hadn't spoken to anyone. Not Sabine. Not Lilith. Not even the wind that moved through the trees like a restless ghost.

I had simply walked.

Now I sat alone at the edge of the sleeping camp, my legs curled beneath me in the cool grass. The earth felt cold even through the layers of my skirt, damp with dew and night air. Behind me the circus slept in quiet pockets of warmth—lanterns glowing dimly beside tents, embers breathing low in fire pits that had burned bright only hours before.

Beyond that glow, the trees waited.

Tall. Dark. Silent silhouettes cut sharply against the sky.

The stars hung above them like scattered diamonds, watching.

My hands trembled in my lap, though I didn't feel afraid. Not truly. The feeling inside me was something stranger than fear, something deeper.

I felt untethered.

Not a daughter.

Not entirely human.

Not something that had simply been born into the world the way other children were.

Given.

Hidden.

Frozen like a story pressed between the pages of time itself.

I closed my eyes and saw her again.

Aeloria.

Madame Thorne.

But not the woman I had come to know—the quiet ruler of the circus with eyes like old storms and a presence that bent the air around her. I saw the child she had once been. Barefoot in wild grass. Flowers wilting beneath her touch. A girl who saw the future before she knew what prophecy meant.

I saw the slave.

The child bride.

The woman bound to a king who feared her power but wanted it all the same.

And then I saw the mother.

The moment she hid her child in the forest. The moment she walked into fire knowing she might never see that child again.

The flame behind my ribs flickered hotter.

All of it—every memory, every wound, every spark of magic—lived inside me now.

The grass crunched softly behind me.

I didn't turn.

Lilith's voice drifted through the quiet night air, warm and careful. "We were waiting for you. Thought maybe you'd gone."

I let out a slow breath. "I did," I murmured. "Just not far."

For a moment neither of them spoke. I could feel their presence behind me like warmth at my back—steady, patient, letting me come to them on my own terms.

Then Lilith asked gently, "Do you want to be alone?"

The answer rose immediately in my chest.

No.

But the word caught somewhere in my throat before it could reach my lips.

Sabine crouched beside me instead, moving quietly through the grass. The faint scent of smoke and salt clung to her hair, comforting in a way I didn't know how to explain. She held out a small tin cup toward me.

"We brought you this," she said softly.

I took it without thinking.

The metal was warm in my hands, the drink inside darker than I expected. I lifted it to my lips and took a small sip. The taste was bitter at first—strong herbs and something earthy—but sweetness followed at the end, like honey lingering on the tongue.

For a long moment none of us spoke.

The circus breathed quietly behind us.

"I don't know who I am anymore," I whispered finally.

Sabine didn't hesitate.

"You're Evelyn."

The certainty in her voice made something twist painfully in my chest.

"Am I?" I asked.

Lilith moved closer then, lowering herself to the grass beside us. Her knee brushed mine, a quiet anchor in the shifting storm of my thoughts.

"You're who you choose to be," she said gently. "You don't owe the past anything."

"But it owes me," I said before I could stop myself.

The bitterness in my voice surprised even me.

Neither of them flinched.

Lilith reached for my hand, her fingers sliding through mine until our palms fit together easily. The warmth of her skin grounded me in a way that felt almost magical.

"I wrote about her," I said suddenly.

The words spilled out before I could decide whether I wanted to share them.

"In my journal," I continued, my voice barely louder than the wind in the trees. "Before I ever came here. Before I knew any of you. I drew women with wings. I wrote stories about storms that could be summoned with a scream. Fire that bloomed instead of burned."

My throat tightened.

"It was all real."

Sabine's eyes softened.

"The things I saw," I whispered. "The dreams I had… were they visions? Were they memories from her? Things she wanted me to remember?"

They didn't answer immediately.

Instead Sabine reached out and brushed her knuckles lightly along my cheek, her touch impossibly gentle.

"You were never crazy," she said softly.

Her voice carried the quiet weight of truth.

"You were remembering."

A wind moved through the trees then, stronger this time, rustling leaves and bending tall grass in a silver wave beneath the moonlight.

Somewhere in the distance a wolf howled.

The sound curled through the forest and settled deep in my bones.

And suddenly the truth rose to my lips before I could stop it.

"She gave me away."

The words tasted raw and fragile.

"She gave me away."

Lilith squeezed my hand.

"She protected you," she said.

"She could have kept you," Sabine added quietly. "Raised you here. Raised you in magic and danger and everything that comes with it."

"But she didn't."

"No," Lilith said. "Because she wanted you to choose."

I looked down into the empty cup resting in my hands.

"She wanted me to have a normal life."

"She wanted you to have the chance at one," Sabine corrected gently.

"She didn't want you caged the way she was."

Something inside my chest shifted then.

Not breaking.

Not shattering.

Something deeper.

Like bones settling back into their proper place after years of quiet misalignment.

"I feel her," I said slowly.

Both of them looked at me.

"It's like… a string humming inside my chest," I tried to explain. "A thread pulled tight between us. I feel her watching. Even when she isn't there."

Sabine nodded slowly.

"Good."

The word caught me off guard.

"Good?" I echoed.

Her expression darkened slightly.

"Because there are darker things watching too."

My breath caught.

"What do you mean?"

Lilith's smile appeared then, but it didn't reach her eyes.

"Being born of old magic," she said quietly, "means old magic remembers you."

The wind stirred again.

The trees whispered.

"And not all of it is kind."

A chill ran down my spine.

I rose slowly to my feet, brushing damp grass from my skirt as the stars above pulsed faintly like distant eyes.

"I want to know everything," I said.

"How to use it. What it means. All of it."

Sabine stood beside me.

Lilith followed a heartbeat later.

For a moment the three of us simply stood there beneath the wide night sky, the circus breathing quietly behind us.

Lilith tilted her head slightly.

"Then you'd better get some rest," she said.

Sabine's gaze held mine as she added quietly, "Tomorrow we start."

And for the first time since leaving Thorne's tent, the uncertainty inside me didn't feel like something to fear.

It felt like the beginning of something vast.

Chapter Thirty-Three

Under the Big Top

The Unveiling

The sky above the great canvas of the circus was still bruised with the last shadows of night, a deep indigo bleeding slowly toward dawn. Most of the world remained asleep beneath it—tents quiet, lanterns dim, fire pits reduced to glowing embers that breathed softly in the dark.

But something inside me had already risen.

It was a hum at first, subtle and persistent, like a distant chord vibrating somewhere deep in my bones. A whisper moved behind my eyes, tugging gently at my awareness, urging me toward wakefulness long before the rest of the camp stirred.

It was more than restlessness.

It was knowing.

I lay still beneath the patchwork blankets for a moment, staring at the canvas ceiling of the tent above me. The fabric shifted faintly in the wind, shadows drifting across its seams like slow-moving clouds.

I wasn't just Evelyn anymore.

The realization didn't frighten me the way it might have only days ago. Instead, it settled inside my chest with a quiet, steady certainty.

I was hers.

And I was still me.

Both truths existed at once, braided together like strands of fire and smoke.

I slipped carefully from beneath the blankets so I wouldn't wake Sabine or Lilith. The air inside the tent was cool against my skin, carrying the faint scent of ash and lavender that always seemed to linger here. I pulled on my boots, tying them with fingers that felt strangely steady, and stepped outside into the quiet morning.

The grass was wet with dew, cool beneath the soles of my boots as I crossed the sleeping camp.

Most of the circus still slumbered. Tents stood like silent guardians around the clearing, their canvas walls glowing faintly in the moonlight. A few distant horses shifted in their stalls, the soft rustle of hay the only sound breaking the stillness.

But beyond the dying fire rings, a single lantern burned bright.

Waiting.

Madame Thorne sat at the edge of the clearing, exactly where the lantern's glow spilled into the darkness of the surrounding trees. She looked as though she had been there for hours, perfectly still, her long dark coat pooling around her like spilled ink.

Maybe she had been waiting that long.

Maybe she had always known I would come.

"You're ready," she said.

It wasn't a question.

I nodded once as I approached, the certainty inside me settling deeper with each step.

"Good," she said softly. "Then you'll learn quickly."

She motioned to the space beside her.

"Sit."

I lowered myself to the ground beside her, the cool earth pressing through my skirt as I folded my legs beneath me. Up close, I could see the shapes she had carved into the dirt between us—symbols drawn with careful precision, lines that twisted and curved into patterns I didn't recognize.

And yet, somewhere deep inside me, they felt familiar.

Like a language I had almost forgotten.

Thorne's fingers continued to move across the soil, completing one final symbol before she reached into the pocket of her coat and withdrew a small glass vial. The liquid inside shimmered faintly in the lantern light, silver and alive.

She poured it into her palm and held it out to me.

"Drink."

I didn't hesitate.

The liquid was cool when it touched my tongue, metallic and strangely sweet at the same time. The moment I swallowed, the world shifted.

The stars above us rippled.

The wind stopped mid-breath, the trees freezing in place as though someone had pressed pause on the entire world.

For a heartbeat everything held perfectly still.

Then reality cracked open.

I blinked—and suddenly I was standing.

But not where I had been sitting.

I turned slowly and saw my body still seated beside Thorne in the dirt, eyes closed, lips parted slightly as though caught between breaths.

A strange, weightless sensation flooded through me.

I lifted my hand instinctively, watching in wonder as it moved through the air like drifting smoke.

"Welcome to the threshold," Thorne's voice said.

But her lips hadn't moved.

Her voice came from everywhere—from the windless air, from the lantern light, from the silent earth beneath my feet.

I spun slowly in place, my heart pounding even though I no longer felt the familiar weight of my body.

"This is astral projection," she continued calmly. "Your soul stepping beyond the cage of your skin. Few can do it."

Her voice softened slightly.

"Fewer survive it."

A strange laugh escaped me, light and breathless.

"I'm not afraid," I said.

And to my surprise, it was true.

"You shouldn't be," Thorne replied. "You were born for this."

The space around me bent gently, like heat rising from sun-warmed stone. Something tugged at me then—a pull, subtle but undeniable.

A thread tightening somewhere deep in my chest.

The world shifted again.

And suddenly I knew where I was going.

My house.

The kitchen window.

The crooked wooden fence that had always leaned slightly to one side.

The dim dining room where so many silent meals had passed between forced prayers and judgmental glances.

I drifted forward without walking.

Walls meant nothing here.

I felt her before I saw her.

My mother.

She sat alone at the kitchen table, her back stiff, her fingers twitching nervously beside the rosary beads coiled around her wrist. A single candle burned in front of her, its light flickering wildly against the walls.

She was muttering to herself.

Or perhaps praying.

Or perhaps trying to convince herself that the silence around her meant safety.

I glided closer.

Her head jerked upward suddenly.

Her eyes scanned the room wildly.

She couldn't see me.

But she felt me.

I watched the moment the realization settled into her bones.

Her gaze followed the space where I hovered, her breath quickening.

"Devil," she whispered hoarsely.

Her fingers tightened around the rosary.

"Satan, is that you?"

Something dark and gleaming stirred inside my chest.

I said nothing.

I didn't need to.

Instead I let my presence expand slowly through the room like creeping frost.

Cold.

Silent.

Unavoidable.

Her chair scraped violently across the floor as she stumbled backward. One of the crosses hanging on the wall behind her rattled loose and crashed to the floor.

Her lips moved frantically, prayers spilling from her mouth in panicked whispers.

"Deliver us from evil—deliver us from—"

Her voice cracked.

I smiled.

And then I allowed the thread pulling me home to tighten once more.

The world snapped back into place like a door slamming shut.

Air rushed into my lungs in a sharp gasp as I collapsed forward onto my hands.

Thorne's hand settled firmly on my shoulder, steadying me.

"You found your tether," she said quietly.

There was something almost proud in her voice.

"Most get lost the first time."

My chest rose and fell rapidly as I tried to catch my breath.

"She saw me," I whispered.

"Or she felt me."

Thorne's expression didn't change.

"Good."

I looked up at her then, a new spark burning behind my eyes.

"I want to do more," I said.

The words felt solid. Certain.

"I want to show her what she's done. I want her to feel it. Every night. Every breath."

The lantern light flickered across Thorne's face as she turned fully toward me.

Her gaze sharpened, ancient and unwavering.

"Are you prepared for what that means?" she asked.

Her voice held no judgment—only truth.

"Revenge takes more than power. It requires precision. Intention. Discipline."

She leaned slightly closer.

"And once you begin walking that path… it carves its name into you."

I didn't look away.

"She carved her name into me long ago."

Silence hung between us for a long moment.

Then Thorne nodded once.

Slowly.

"Then," she said, rising to her feet, "let me show you the blade."

Chapter Thirty-Four

Under the Big Top

Practice Before the Show

By evening the circus had awakened fully, stretching itself from the quiet hush of dawn into the electric anticipation that always came before a performance. Lanterns flickered to life one by one along the ropes and tent poles, their golden glow scattering across the sawdust-covered grounds. Somewhere near the front gates a vendor roasted peanuts over a small iron drum, the warm scent drifting lazily through the air and mixing with the familiar smells of canvas, woodsmoke, and animals.

Performers moved through the pathways between tents like restless spirits preparing for their rituals. The tightrope walkers practiced slow, careful steps along a low training wire strung between two poles. The fire-eaters sat cross-legged beside a lantern, polishing their metal torches until they gleamed. Laughter and quiet chatter drifted through the camp, mingling with the distant tuning of instruments beneath the big top.

The circus was alive.

But tonight felt different.

I could feel it in the steady pulse beneath my skin, in the strange hum of energy that lingered behind my ribs. I had woken to power that morning—raw and unfamiliar, like a storm gathering somewhere deep inside my bones. The day had been spent learning how to bend it, how to listen to the quiet pull of magic moving through me like a second heartbeat.

Now the time had come to wield it.

"Practice ring," Lilith called.

Her voice cut cleanly through the growing noise of the camp. She stood a few paces away beneath the lantern light, motioning for me to follow. Her arms were bare tonight, the ink that lived beneath her skin shifting faintly in the warm glow of the lamps. The dark tattoos curled and breathed across her shoulders like living vines, responding subtly to the movement of her muscles.

Her eyes held that same quiet spark they always did when something interested her.

"Time to see what you're really made of," she added.

I followed her through the maze of tents toward the empty training ring at the far edge of the grounds. The canvas walls of the big top loomed above us like a sleeping giant, its ropes humming faintly in the evening breeze.

Sabine was already waiting in the center of the ring.

Her bright hair had been pulled back into a loose braid, though a few stubborn strands had escaped and glowed softly in the lantern light. A thin ribbon of flame curled lazily around her fingertips, dancing along her skin without leaving so much as a mark.

The fire reflected in the knowing smirk on her lips.

Madame Thorne stood just beyond the circle of sawdust, arms folded loosely across her chest as she watched us. Her expression was calm and unreadable, but her eyes missed nothing.

"Again," she said simply.

Her voice carried the quiet authority of someone who had watched centuries unfold and still demanded more.

"Push harder this time."

I stepped into the center of the ring and closed my eyes for a moment, letting the sounds of the circus fade into the background. The world narrowed to the steady rhythm of my breath and the pulse of magic humming beneath my skin.

I reached inward.

The heat responded immediately.

It wasn't just fire—not anymore. It was sensation. Memory. Emotion braided together into something stronger than any single element could be alone.

Fury burned there, sharp and bright.

So did joy.

Desire flickered quietly at the edges, soft and dangerous.

And somewhere beneath all of it lived love.

Lilith stepped forward slowly until she stood just in front of me. Without speaking she reached out and brushed her fingers lightly against mine.

The moment our skin touched, the power surged.

Her tattoos glowed faintly, the dark ink shifting into subtle motion beneath her skin. I felt the magic inside her like a living thing— ancient and curious—and something inside me answered in kind.

It stretched.

Expanded.

Bloomed outward.

"Do you feel it?" Lilith asked quietly.

My breath caught.

"I feel everything."

The words escaped me before I could think about them.

I closed my eyes.

The world shifted instantly.

It felt like lifting—not just physically, but from somewhere deeper than bone or flesh. My awareness slipped free from my body like mist rising from warm earth. For a moment there was nothing but weightlessness and quiet wonder.

Then the thread inside my chest tightened.

I didn't need to choose where to go.

My heart already had.

Margaret.

The world bent around me again.

When it settled, I found her exactly where I had imagined.

She sat alone beside the hearth in her uncle's narrow sitting room, the fire burning low enough that the shadows swallowed most of the space. A small Bible rested in her lap, clutched so tightly between her hands that her knuckles had turned pale.

She looked smaller somehow.

Thinner.

The warmth that had once lived in her eyes had faded into something fragile and haunted.

I drifted closer.

At first she didn't notice me.

Then her head lifted suddenly.

Her breath caught.

For a long moment she simply stared at the empty space where I hovered, her eyes searching the air as if trying to decide whether what she felt was real.

Her lips parted.

But no sound came out.

"It was all real," I whispered.

My voice moved through the room like a quiet echo.

"The things I wrote in my journal," I continued softly. "The women with wings. The storms I screamed into being. I thought they were just stories once."

I took another slow step forward.

"They were visions."

Margaret's fingers tightened around the edges of her Bible. Tears gathered slowly along her lashes, trembling there as if they were unsure whether they were allowed to fall.

"When you left me that night in the church," I said gently, "you left me to face her alone."

The memory flickered through my mind—the shock in her eyes, the way she had run when my mother's voice shattered the quiet of the chapel.

"Do you know what she did to me after that?"

Margaret didn't answer.

But she didn't look away either.

"I loved you," I told her quietly.

The words were easier to say now than they had ever been before.

"I still do. In some small way."

The ache that once lived behind those words had softened into something steadier.

"And I forgive you."

Her breath hitched.

"Because your leaving pushed me here," I continued. "To them. To this life."

I lifted my hand slowly.

The air between us shimmered faintly as the magic within me stirred.

Margaret hesitated before raising her own hand in response. Her fingers trembled as she reached toward the space where my presence hovered.

For one fleeting moment, I let her feel it.

Warmth.

Life.

Not a ghost.

Something new.

Her eyes widened.

Then I pulled away.

The thread in my chest tightened again.

The world folded inward.

And suddenly I was back.

My lungs filled with night air in a sharp gasp as my awareness slammed back into my body.

Sabine was beside me instantly, her hands steady on my shoulders as she caught me before my knees could buckle.

"You alright?" she asked quietly.

I nodded, blinking as the world settled back into focus around me.

"I was with Margaret."

Lilith stepped closer, studying my face carefully.

"She saw you?"

"She did," I said.

The memory of her wide eyes still lingered in my mind.

"And she understood."

Sabine's flame flickered slightly in her palm.

"Good," she murmured.

I looked between them both then, feeling something fierce and bright coil inside my chest.

A storm waiting to break.

"And now I want to use it," I said.

The words felt powerful just speaking them aloud.

"All of it."

Sabine lifted her hand, the small flame dancing in her palm like a secret meant only for us.

"Then," she said with a quiet smile, "let's get you ready for tonight."

The twilight outside deepened as we moved back toward the performance ring. Lanterns brightened, music swelled somewhere inside the big tent, and the distant murmur of gathering crowds drifted across the circus grounds.

From the shadows beyond the ring, Madame Thorne watched us.

Her expression remained calm.

But there was pride in her eyes.

Tonight, I wouldn't simply step onto the stage.

Tonight, the world would finally meet the storm I had always been becoming.

Chapter Thirty-Five

Under the Big Top

Smoke and Recognition

The road had worn him thin.

Days of travel had carved exhaustion into his bones, grinding him down until every step felt heavier than the last. His boots were caked with layers of dried mud and dust from roads that seemed to stretch endlessly across the countryside. Rain had soaked his coat more times than he could count, leaving the thick wool stiff and weathered against his shoulders.

But none of that mattered.

Grief had weighed more than the miles ever could.

He had followed rumors through towns that barely remembered their own names. Some places were bustling with travelers and wagons; others were nothing more than a handful of buildings leaning against the wind. Everywhere he went, he asked the same question.

Had anyone seen a circus?

A strange one.

A place where impossible things happened.

Sometimes people laughed at him.

Sometimes they told stories.

Stories about a girl who appeared in smoke and vanished before anyone could reach her. Stories about a woman who sang storms into existence beneath the great tent. Stories about lightning dancing in someone's hands.

Most pointed him toward empty fields where wagons had once stood only days before.

Always too late.

Always just behind.

But tonight something was different.

Tonight there was a name.

Cirque de Lune Noire.

It hadn't come from drunken gossip or exaggerated tales shared over tavern tables. No one had whispered it to him like a rumor meant to fade with the morning.

He had felt it.

Deep in his chest.

A strange pull, like a bell ringing somewhere inside his ribs.

Something in the world had shifted.

And he knew—without understanding how—that it had something to do with Evelyn.

The circus stood just beyond the edge of town, its towering tents glowing faintly against the darkening sky. Lanterns hung from tall wooden poles, swaying gently in the wind and casting long golden ribbons of light across the grass.

Music drifted faintly from within.

The air smelled of roasted peanuts, sawdust, and something stranger—something floral and warm, like jasmine carried on smoke.

He stood at the entrance for a long moment before stepping forward.

The man selling tickets watched him carefully as he approached.

John Ashmoor's hands trembled slightly as he reached for his wallet. The coins clinked softly together as he counted them out and placed them on the small wooden counter.

The ticket seller didn't ask questions.

He simply nodded once, slowly, as if he understood more than he let on.

Then he handed John the ticket.

Inside, the tent was unlike anything he had imagined.

The space glowed with a strange, living light—not the dull flicker of gas lamps or candle flames. This light shimmered softly, drifting across the velvet curtains and polished brass railings like something alive.

The audience buzzed with excitement.

Families leaned forward eagerly in their seats. Children whispered and pointed toward the empty ring at the center of the tent. Musicians tuned their instruments somewhere in the shadows above the rafters.

John found a seat halfway up the wooden stands.

His eyes moved constantly.

Every performer.

Every assistant.

Every shadow that slipped behind the curtains.

The show began.

Acrobats launched themselves through the air with impossible grace, spinning and twisting like falling stars. A woman in silver walked barefoot through a storm of spinning blades, each knife missing her skin by no more than a breath. A man dissolved into smoke before the audience's eyes, reappearing moments later inside a cage built from curved white bones.

The crowd gasped.

They clapped.

They laughed in disbelief.

But John barely noticed any of it.

His attention searched every face, every movement.

Looking for her.

Minutes passed.

Then more.

A knot of despair tightened slowly inside his chest.

Another dead end, he thought.

Another story that would lead nowhere.

Then the ringmaster's voice rolled through the tent.

Deep.

Slow.

Like thunder gathering across still water.

"Ladies and gentlemen," the voice said, "prepare yourselves."

The audience quieted instantly.

"For the marvel cloaked in shadow and flame."

A hush spread through the tent like snowfall.

"The storm-singer."

The musicians fell silent.

"The dream walker."

Even the restless children stopped whispering.

"The girl…"

The lanterns dimmed.

"In smoke."

For a single heartbeat, nothing happened.

Then the ring filled with silver mist.

Smoke poured across the sawdust floor in curling waves, sliding through the ring like living serpents. It rose slowly, climbing higher and higher until the entire center of the tent disappeared behind a wall of swirling silver.

Gasps rippled through the audience.

The smoke thickened.

A breath passed.

And then—

She appeared.

Suspended in the center of the storm.

Evelyn.

She floated effortlessly above the ring, her feet resting on nothing but air. Her long hair hung loose around her shoulders, drifting as if caught in a wind no one else could feel. The lantern light caught the faint violet glow in her eyes, making them shine like distant stars.

The smoke wrapped around her body like a living cloak.

When she raised her hand, it burst outward in a sudden explosion of color.

Stars.

Moons.

Flashes of burning gold.

The shapes spun outward in dazzling spirals above the audience.

Gasps filled the tent.

John stood.

He didn't even realize he had done it.

His heart hammered violently in his chest.

She turned slowly in the air.

As if she had sensed him.

Their eyes met.

Across the impossible distance.

For a single fragile moment, the world narrowed to nothing but that connection.

It's her.

The realization hit him like lightning.

His daughter.

Alive.

Evelyn faltered for the briefest breath.

Then the performer returned.

The smoke twisted again, shaping itself into a flock of silver birds. They soared above the audience, scattering tiny sparks that shimmered like falling starlight. A storm cloud gathered above the ring, thunder rumbling faintly beneath the canvas roof.

Evelyn lifted both hands.

Lightning cracked between her fingers.

The crowd leaned forward, spellbound.

Then she screamed.

Not in fear.

Not in pain.

It was something deeper.

Release.

Fury.

Freedom.

Power.

The sound tore through the tent like a breaking storm, dissolving into a rush of wind that swept across the audience. Hair lifted. Clothing rustled. The entire crowd seemed to inhale at once.

Then—

She vanished.

The smoke collapsed inward and disappeared.

The ring stood empty.

For one stunned second the audience remained frozen.

Then the tent erupted.

Applause thundered through the air.

People leapt to their feet, cheering and shouting in disbelief.

John clapped with them.

Harder than anyone.

His hands stung.

His eyes blurred.

She was real.

His daughter was real.

Long after the final applause faded, he remained seated in the quiet tent.

One by one the lanterns dimmed.

The crowd drifted away.

Eventually he was alone.

A soft voice spoke beside him.

"Mr. Ashmoor."

He turned.

Madam Thorne stood there in deep crimson robes, her presence quiet but impossible to ignore. A velvet top hat rested atop her dark hair, casting a shadow over eyes that looked older than winter itself.

"Come with me," she said gently.

He didn't hesitate.

She led him through a maze of narrow corridors behind the stage. Velvet curtains brushed against his shoulders as they passed. Performers laughed softly over mugs of steaming tea. Someone practiced a slow violin melody in the distance.

They passed mirrors that reflected nothing at all.

At last Thorne stopped beside a heavy velvet curtain.

She turned toward him.

"She's been waiting for you," she said quietly.

Her voice softened.

"Even when she told herself she wasn't."

John swallowed hard and nodded.

Thorne lifted the curtain.

Inside, a lantern flickered gently in the dim space.

Evelyn stood alone in the center of the room, still dressed in her performance costume. The plum and silver fabric shimmered faintly in the lantern light, smoke still clinging to the edges of her hair like the memory of magic.

She looked up.

Their eyes met.

John stepped forward slowly.

Then stopped.

"Evelyn," he whispered.

She didn't answer.

Not yet.

The silence between them stretched tight and electric.

Like the moment just before lightning strikes.

Chapter Thirty-Six

Under the Big Top

Reunion Beneath the Moon

The performance had ended, but the energy of it still clung to the air like lingering thunder after a storm. Even backstage, where the lanterns burned lower and the sounds of the crowd faded into distant echoes, the magic still hummed softly beneath my skin.

My breath came in short, uneven bursts as I stood in the dim corridor behind the big top. Wisps of silver smoke still drifted lazily around my fingertips, the last remnants of the power I had summoned in the ring. My heart pounded so hard I could feel it in my throat, in my wrists, in the quiet spaces between my ribs.

Then I saw him.

My father.

He stood at the far end of the corridor, just inside the velvet curtain that separated the performers from the audience pathways. For a moment he didn't move, as though the sight of me had rooted him to the floor.

Madame Thorne stood beside him, her hand resting lightly on his shoulder. She guided him forward a few steps, then released him and quietly stepped away, leaving us alone in the flickering lantern light.

For a long heartbeat neither of us spoke.

The silence stretched between us like a fragile thread.

Then his voice broke it.

"Evie?"

The sound of my name in his voice shattered something inside me. It cracked like old wood splitting beneath pressure, carrying with it years of regret, relief, and longing all tangled together.

I nodded, but my throat was too tight to form words.

He crossed the space between us in a few uneven steps, his boots scraping softly against the wooden boards beneath our feet. When he reached me, his hands rose hesitantly—as if he were afraid that I might vanish like smoke if he touched me.

Then his palms cupped my face.

They trembled.

"My God," he whispered softly. "Look at you."

Tears spilled down my cheeks before I could stop them.

"You came."

The words escaped in a fragile breath.

"I've been looking for you every day," he said. His voice shook, but there was a fierce determination beneath it. "Every town, every circus I could find. I followed every rumor about a girl who danced with fire or vanished in smoke."

He swallowed hard, his eyes searching my face as though trying to memorize every detail.

"I knew," he said quietly. "I don't know how, but I knew I had to find you."

My hands closed around his wrists, grounding myself in the warmth of his skin.

"I didn't think you'd believe me," I admitted.

For a moment guilt flickered across his face like a passing shadow.

"I didn't," he said honestly.

His hands slipped from my cheeks to take both of mine, holding them tightly between his own.

"And I hate myself for that," he continued. "For not listening when you tried to tell me what was happening. For not seeing what she was doing to you."

His voice broke slightly.

"Evelyn… I failed you. I should have protected you."

I shook my head quickly, squeezing his hands.

"You didn't fail me," I said softly. "You just didn't know."

His eyes searched mine again, as if trying to understand the girl standing before him.

"The night you ran away," he said slowly, "I felt it."

I frowned slightly.

"What do you mean?"

"I was working late," he explained. "At the rail office. Going through freight ledgers. And suddenly this… ache hit me right here."

He pressed a hand lightly against the center of his chest.

"It felt like something inside me cracked open. Like ice breaking. I didn't know what it meant then, but I knew something was wrong."

His jaw tightened.

"And when I got home, you were gone."

The pain in his voice was sharp enough to cut through the quiet corridor.

"She wouldn't even look me in the eye," he continued quietly. "I asked her why she hadn't written me, why she hadn't sent a message when you disappeared."

His mouth twisted with bitterness.

"She said she didn't care that you were gone. Said it was one less sinner she needed to try and save."

The words struck something deep inside me, and I flinched without meaning to.

His hands tightened around mine immediately.

"Evelyn," he said gently, "she told me things I didn't want to believe. But now… now I see it. You were telling the truth all along."

My voice felt fragile when I answered.

"She locked me in the cellar."

The memory flickered through my mind—the cold dirt floor, the rope biting into my wrists, my mother's voice echoing through the door as she prayed for my soul.

"She said I had to stay there until they came for me," I continued quietly. "Men from St. Vincent's Restoration Home for Girls. She said they would cleanse my soul."

My father's face went pale.

"My God," he whispered.

His grip tightened again, as if he needed to feel that I was truly standing there in front of him.

"My Evie," he murmured. "I'm so sorry."

His voice trembled with emotion.

"If I had known—I should have listened, I should have believed you"

"I found out who I really am," I said gently, interrupting him before the guilt could swallow him whole.

He looked into my eyes with steady determination.

"I don't care," he said firmly.

The certainty in his voice made my breath catch.

"I don't care where you came from. I don't care if we don't share blood."

His hand rose again to brush a tear from my cheek.

"You are my daughter, Evelyn," he said softly.

"And I love you more than anything in this world."

The words broke something open inside me.

All the weight I had carried—the fear, the loneliness, the years of wondering whether I had ever truly been loved—collapsed at once.

My knees gave out.

I fell into his arms as sobs tore free from my chest.

He wrapped his arms around me immediately, holding me close the way he had when I was small. The way he used to when nightmares woke me in the middle of the night and monsters still lived safely under beds instead of behind locked cellar doors.

"I love you too," I cried into his shoulder.

We stood like that for a long time.

The lantern beside us flickered softly.

Somewhere in the distance the circus musicians played a slow, quiet tune beneath the canvas roof.

Eventually I pulled back slightly, wiping my face with the back of my hand.

"There's someone I want you to meet," I said.

I turned toward the shadows at the edge of the corridor.

Lilith and Sabine stepped forward slowly, their movements respectful and quiet.

They had been watching the entire time.

"These are—" I hesitated, then smiled softly. "They're more than friends."

Sabine stood with her usual confidence, though the faint glow of fire still curled around her fingertips like a living secret. Lilith stood beside her, arms folded loosely, the dark ink of her tattoos shifting gently beneath her skin.

"They found me," I said. "When I had nowhere else to go. They showed me I was never broken."

My voice softened.

"That I was magic."

I reached for both of their hands.

"And I love them. Both of them."

My father looked at them carefully.

Sabine's flame flickered in the dim light.

Lilith's steady gaze held his without fear.

For a moment he simply studied them.

Then he smiled.

"Then I owe you both more than I can ever say," he said sincerely. "Thank you… for loving my daughter."

Lilith's expression softened slightly.

Sabine's usual smirk faded into something warmer.

"She's easy to love," Lilith said gently.

My father let out a quiet breath.

"I still can't believe what I saw tonight," he admitted, glancing back toward the tent. "The way you moved in the air. The things you can do."

"I'm still learning," I said with a small smile.

"Still becoming."

At that moment Madame Thorne stepped forward from the shadows, her dark coat trailing softly behind her.

Her eyes glinted with quiet approval.

"Evelyn," she said gently, "I would like to offer your father a place here with us."

My father turned toward her, surprised.

"Not as a performer," she continued calmly. "But as family. As someone who can travel with us, help where he wishes, and remain close to the daughter he searched so long to find."

Her gaze moved between us both.

"If that is what you would like."

I looked up at my father.

He didn't hesitate.

"Yes," he said immediately. "If you'll have me."

His eyes softened as he looked at me again.

"If you want me here."

I nodded.

And something warm bloomed quietly in my chest.

All the love I had spent so many years longing for.

All the love I had feared might never belong to me.

It was here now.

We weren't just surviving anymore.

We were healing.

Together.

Chapter Thirty-Seven

Under the Big Top

The Feast Before the Fire

The sun had long since slipped below the horizon, leaving the sky washed in deep indigo and fading streaks of molten gold. Night gathered slowly around the circus grounds, settling like velvet over the sprawling tents and winding pathways of Cirque de Lune Noire. Lanterns swayed gently from twisted iron poles planted throughout the fairgrounds, their warm glow dancing across the dew-kissed grass. Each flicker of light cast shifting shadows that moved like living things along the canvas walls. Music drifted through the evening air—soft violin strings tangled with the distant beat of a drum—and somewhere nearby someone laughed loudly enough to send a ripple of joy through the night.

The warmth of my reunion with my father still pulsed steadily inside my chest as we walked together through the glowing paths between the tents. He moved slowly, his gaze constantly shifting as he tried to take in the impossible world unfolding around him. Performers passed us with friendly nods and raised mugs, their silhouettes cutting through the lantern light like living pieces of some strange and beautiful dream. From one nearby rehearsal tent came a sudden burst of flame, bright and quick as lightning, followed by the crackle of Sabine's laughter as she practiced. My father paused to watch the glow flicker through the canvas before shaking his head in quiet amazement.

"I still can't believe it," he murmured after a moment, his voice filled with wonder. "It's like stepping into a dream."

"It was a dream," I replied softly, watching the light ripple across the grass. "One I never thought I'd be allowed to have."

We wandered through the heart of the circus grounds until the wide canvas walls of the dining tent appeared ahead of us, glowing warmly from within. The scent of food drifted outward in rich waves—slow-cooked stew, roasted vegetables, fresh bread still steaming in wicker baskets. Inside, long wooden tables had already been set, lanterns hanging low above them like captured stars. The moment we stepped through the entrance, conversations slowed just enough for people to notice us before swelling again into cheers and greetings. Voices called my name from every direction. Glasses lifted in celebration. Performers who had once terrified me when I first arrived here now welcomed my father as though he had always belonged among them.

He was ushered to a seat almost immediately, a mug of cider placed in his hands before he could protest. Somehow he found himself sitting beside Madame Thorne at the head of the long table, looking slightly overwhelmed as the tattooed man with the snake curled around his wrist raised a toast in his direction. Across the table, the bearded lady cracked a joke that sent half the room into laughter, while the Knife Twins sat side by side moving in perfect mirrored motions as they ate. My father leaned closer to me after a moment, his voice quiet beneath the rising hum of conversation.

"You found a family," he whispered.

"I did," I said, glancing around the table at the faces illuminated by lantern light. "And I found myself."

Dinner unfolded in a joyful chaos of clinking silverware, stories traded across the table, and music drifting in from somewhere outside the tent. Plates passed from hand to hand, mugs were refilled without asking, and the circus slowly settled into the warm rhythm of shared celebration. By the time the dishes were cleared away, the room had softened into the comfortable quiet that follows a good meal. I found myself seated between Lilith and Sabine, both warm against my sides. Sabine's fingers brushed mine beneath the table while Lilith leaned back in her chair, her tattoos shifting faintly beneath the lantern glow.

My father leaned forward slightly then, his expression thoughtful. "Can I ask you something?" he said. I nodded, already sensing what was coming. "What happened… with Margaret? I heard the murmurs of the towns folk."

The question tightened something in my chest. For a moment I stared at my hands before answering. "She ran," I said quietly. "When my mother found us in the church, she panicked. She ran and didn't look back." My father's expression darkened with sorrow. "I'm sorry," he murmured. I took a slow breath before continuing. "I loved her. I think I always will in some small way. But when she left me there—alone with my mother—that was the worst moment of my life. I thought I was disgusting. I thought I deserved everything that came after."

"You didn't," my father said fiercely, the certainty in his voice making my throat tighten.

"I know that now," I replied softly. "But back then I couldn't see it. It took Lilith and Sabine to show me the truth. To remind me that real love doesn't run." Sabine squeezed my hand gently beneath the table while Lilith's quiet smile held a fierce kind of pride.

At the head of the table, Madame Thorne rose slowly to her feet, and the room fell silent almost at once. Her gaze moved across the gathered performers before settling on me with quiet intensity. "Evelyn," she said, raising her glass. "You have come home." A murmur of agreement rippled through the tent, but Thorne continued before the noise could rise again. "Yet we believe it may be time for something more. It may be time for you to return to the place that tried to erase you—not as a girl in hiding, but as the woman you have become."

The words sent a shiver through the room. She paused before continuing. "What if we brought Cirque de Lune Noire to your hometown? For one night only. A special performance. An unveiling."

My breath caught in my throat. Lilith leaned closer, her voice low beside my ear. "Let her see you. See what she couldn't kill." Sabine's grin flashed with wicked excitement. "We'll send invitations to everyone in town. Everyone who ever looked the other way." One of the aerialists leaned forward with a mischievous spark in her eyes. "And we'll start haunting her—little things at first. Enough to make sure she comes."

My hands trembled slightly. "You want to put on a show… for my mother?"

"No," Madame Thorne replied, her voice smooth as silk but edged with steel. "We want to put on a reckoning. And you will be the one who delivers it."

I turned slowly toward my father. "Are you okay with this? Truly?" The question hung heavily between us. He looked at me for a long moment before answering.

"You deserve this, Evelyn," he said gently. "I'll help however I can. I'll go back ahead of the circus. I'll tell her I failed—that I searched everywhere and found nothing. And I'll make sure she attends that show."

Emotion swelled painfully in my chest. Madame Thorne lifted her glass again. "Then it is decided. Cirque de Lune Noire will travel to the heart of Evelyn's past, and the town that tried to bury her will see what she has become."

Lilith's voice followed softly. "And her mother will witness the truth."

A slow, steady fire rose inside me as I nodded. This wouldn't be just another performance beneath the big top. It would be something far more powerful. Catharsis. Judgment. Triumph.

Let her see me.

Let them all see.

The girl they tried to silence was about to take center stage.

Chapter Thirty-Eight

Under the Big Top

Ghosts of the Living

The first time I returned to her, it was only a whisper of shadow.

I stood outside my childhood home in my astral form, my presence woven from smoke, memory, and something far older than either of them. The world around me felt thinner here, like reality itself was only loosely stitched together. The house looked smaller than I remembered. The once-neat garden had withered into brittle stalks and tangled weeds, and the porch steps were cracked and splintering beneath years of neglect. Nothing about it felt warm. Nothing about it felt like home. The place hadn't changed much since the night I ran away.

But I had.

Inside the house, she moved through the halls with the same rigid posture I remembered—like a queen presiding over a crumbling kingdom she refused to abandon. My mother's frame was still sturdy, still commanding in its quiet severity, but something in her eyes had changed. There was a flicker there now, something small and uncertain that hadn't existed before.

Fear.

She still followed the same rituals she always had. Every morning she sat at the worn kitchen table where the wood had been rubbed smooth by years of restless prayer. Her Bible lay open to the same marked passages, its pages bent and softened from constant use. Her fingers brushed over the ink as she whispered the verses beneath her breath, as though they were charms meant to hold back something dark pressing against the edges of her life.

"Psalm ninety-one," she murmured softly, her voice steady but thin. "He who dwells in the secret place of the Most High shall abide under the shadow of the Almighty…"

I stood behind her, silent and unseen. She couldn't see me—not yet—but she felt something. I saw it in the way her shoulders tightened, in the faint shiver that ran through her spine.

I breathed once.

The candle burning beside her sputtered violently and went dark.

She froze.

Slowly, her head turned as she looked around the empty room. Her gaze moved across the walls, the doorway, the small kitchen window where pale morning light filtered through the glass.

"In the name of Jesus," she whispered, her voice tightening as her fingers curled around the edge of the table. "Deliver me from evil. I rebuke this presence. I rebuke this devil."

I smiled.

The next night I returned again, but this time I was bolder.

I stood at the foot of her bed and watched her sleep. The room smelled faintly of citrus soap and something else—guilt, perhaps, soaked deep into the wood of the walls. Her breathing rose and fell unevenly as she tossed beneath the blankets. Even in sleep her brow was furrowed, her fingers clutching the thin cross that hung around her neck.

I waited until her breathing slowed.

Until the quiet settled into the room.

Then I whispered.

"If you say your verse loud enough," I murmured softly, "maybe the devil will leave the room."

Her eyes flew open.

She shot upright in the bed with a sharp gasp, her gaze darting wildly across the darkened room.

"Who's there?" she demanded hoarsely.

Her hand tightened around the cross at her throat.

"I bind you in the blood of the Lamb!"

But nothing happened.

The cross did not glow.

No holy light flooded the room.

The air only grew colder.

I drifted closer to the vanity beside the bed and pressed my fingers against the dusty mirror. When I pulled my hand away, a pale smear remained behind in the shape of a crescent moon.

By morning she had called the pastor.

He walked through the house with a small silver bowl, sprinkling holy water across the doorframes and windowsills. He murmured prayers beneath his breath while my mother followed close behind him, clutching her Bible like armor against an unseen war.

She recited the Beatitudes until her voice grew raw.

She whispered verses while she cooked.

While she cleaned.

While she sat alone at the kitchen table long after the sun had gone down.

It didn't help.

Every night, I returned.

Sometimes I sang the hymns she used to force me to sing through the vent while she locked me in the cellar. Other nights I whispered the prayers she made me recite whenever she thought punishment might burn the sin out of me.

"The light shines in the darkness," I murmured once from the hallway outside her bedroom door, "and the darkness has not overcome it."

And yet the darkness was everywhere now.

It followed her through the halls.

It breathed against the back of her neck when she prayed.

It waited quietly in every corner of the house she once ruled so confidently.

By the end of the month she had begun to wither beneath the weight of it. The sharp lines of her face had hollowed. Dark circles shadowed her eyes, and the silver threads in her hair had spread like frost along her temples. She paced through the house constantly, Bible clutched to her chest, her lips moving with endless prayers that never seemed to bring her peace.

The town began to notice.

Whispers traveled quickly through small places like ours.

"She says she's haunted."

"I heard her talking to herself in the street."

"She claims the devil came back for her daughter."

Some said it with pity.

Others said it with quiet satisfaction.

And then the letter arrived.

It came in thick ivory paper sealed with a ribbon of deep crimson wax. The envelope bore elegant lettering that curled across the front like smoke.

An invitation.

A one-night performance.

Cirque de Lune Noire.

A spectacle of wonder and mystery.

A girl in smoke.

A show beyond imagination.

She nearly threw it into the fire without opening it.

But my father had returned by then.

He stood on the porch that evening as the sun sank slowly into the horizon, his shoulders heavy with exhaustion.

"I couldn't find her," he told her quietly. "I searched everywhere."

My mother's jaw tightened.

"She's gone," he continued, his voice weary. "But Thorne… that woman from the circus… she might know something. I heard they're coming through town."

Her eyes flashed with sudden anger.

"She gave me that girl," my mother hissed. "That woman is wicked. She brought this curse upon us."

My father studied her carefully before speaking again.

"Then go."

She stared at him.

"Go to the show," he said gently. "Tell her to take it back. Maybe she can stop whatever this is. Maybe if you face her… this will end."

For a long time my mother said nothing.

Then finally she nodded.

Just once.

Back at the circus camp, the fire crackled softly as the others gathered around it. The flames painted their faces in shades of gold and shadow while the night stretched wide above us.

"She'll come," I said quietly.

Sabine's lips curved into a slow, dangerous smile.

"Then we'd better make sure it's a performance she never forgets."

Lilith reached over and touched my arm, her voice warm with quiet pride.

"No more hiding. No more shadows. You show her who you are now, Evelyn."

Her gaze held mine.

“All of it.”

And I would.

Not just for revenge.

But for liberation.

Chapter Thirty-Nine

Under the Big Top

One Night Only

The circus arrived in the dead of night.

Like a dream—or perhaps a warning—it unfolded beneath a silver-slashed moon, the tents rising slowly from the earth like spirits summoned from sleep. Wagons rolled into the town park where Sunday school children once played, their wheels whispering across the grass while lanterns flickered awake one by one. By the time dawn broke, the town had changed. A striped banner fluttered across the main road. Painted wagons rested beneath the old elm trees. The scent of spice, smoke, and something sweet drifted through the air where there should have been nothing but lilacs and morning dew.

By midday the rumors had begun.

Flyers had been delivered to every doorstep before the sun rose. Some were tucked neatly inside church bulletins. Others were pinned to the cork boards at the grocer or taped crookedly against the windows of the post office. The message was simple, written in elegant curling script that looked almost too beautiful for a place like this.

One Night Only.
Cirque de Lune Noire.
Come See the Girl in Smoke.

No one quite knew what it meant, but curiosity spreads quickly in small towns, especially the kind that have buried their secrets so deeply that the soil itself begins to remember.

By evening the line stretched halfway down the road.

I stood at the edge of the circus grounds watching them arrive, cloaked in a velvet cape lined with shadows. The cool night air moved softly through my hair, catching strands of it so they shimmered faintly in the lantern light. My eyes followed the crowd quietly, steady and calm in a way they had never been before.

Behind me the circus moved with quiet purpose. Lilith adjusted the lantern rigging above the entrance to the big top, her tattooed arms gliding through the ropes and pulleys like she had been born to command light itself. Sabine stood near the ring rehearsing the rhythm of her fire wands, each flick of her wrist sending small blossoms of flame spinning into the night air. Around them the rest of the performers prepared their acts—tightropes being strung high above the ring, mirrors wheeled into place, cages that held creatures too strange and beautiful to be called animals.

Even my father moved among them now.

Earlier that afternoon he had helped the stagehands raise the lantern poles and guide the final wagon into position, working quietly beside them as though he had always belonged here. Now he waited near the entrance of the big top, ready to lead my mother inside when she arrived.

Tonight wasn't only a spectacle.

It was a confrontation wrapped in stardust.

From the edge of the grounds I watched the townspeople enter the tent one by one. Faces I recognized appeared in the lantern glow— neighbors who had once crossed the street when they saw me coming, teachers who had watched silently while whispers followed me through the halls, parents who warned their children not to play with the strange girl who lived at the end of the road.

And then I saw her.

My mother.

She walked slowly toward the entrance of the big top dressed entirely in black, her posture rigid with the same brittle authority she had carried my entire life. The Bible was clutched tightly against her chest like a shield. My father walked beside her as they approached the entrance, speaking softly in a voice that almost sounded like compassion.

Inside the circus tent the music had already begun to rise.

Lanterns dimmed as the crowd settled into their seats, and the air filled with the murmur of anticipation that always comes before a show. When the first drumbeat sounded, the entire tent seemed to pulse with it.

Act by act, the circus unfolded before them.

Sabine stepped into the ring first, her flames spiraling through the darkness like living stories written in fire. Each arc of light painted shapes into the air—dragons and phoenixes, storms and suns—until the crowd gasped with every movement of her hands. Lilith followed, weaving illusions so seamlessly into the performance that silk ribbons became blades of silver light and mirrors shattered into flocks of glass birds that circled the tent before dissolving into nothing.

The audience sat stunned, their disbelief melting slowly into awe.

But the real silence came when Madame Thorne stepped into the center of the ring.

She stood there for a moment without speaking, her crimson coat catching the lantern light as she raised one gloved hand. The music faded almost instantly.

"Tonight," she said, her voice carrying easily through the tent, "you will see more than tricks."

The lanterns dimmed further.

"You will see truth."

A low breath of fog slipped across the floor of the ring, spreading outward like a memory rising from the earth. The audience leaned forward, their whispers fading into complete silence.

Then I stepped forward.

The smoke rose with me, curling around my feet until it lifted me gently from the ground. My body floated weightless above the ring, wrapped in shifting shadows that glowed softly like starlight caught inside fog. When I spoke, my voice carried through the entire tent—not loud, but powerful enough that every person inside felt it.

"This," I said slowly, my gaze sweeping across the crowd, "is who I am."

The smoke behind me began to move, bending itself into shapes that shimmered in the air like living memories.

"The girl you tried to silence."

A cellar door slammed shut inside the fog.

"The girl you abandoned."

A child curled into herself beneath wooden stairs.

"The girl who refused to break."

The memory flared into sudden flame.

Gasps rippled through the audience.

Across the tent my mother sat perfectly still.

Her face had drained of all color. The Bible trembled faintly in her hands as the smoke began to drift toward her, curling around her ankles first, then rising slowly toward her waist like a living thing.

When I spoke again, my voice reached only her.

"Say the verse, Mother."

She jerked violently in her seat, turning her head as though searching for something she could not see.

"Go ahead," I whispered. "Cast the devil out of me."

Her breathing grew sharp and frantic.

The smoke thickened around her chair.

"Repeat it," I murmured, appearing suddenly in the empty aisle beside her. "He that walketh uprightly walketh surely…"

Her hands tightened around the Bible.

"Or is it not working this time?"

The entire tent had gone silent.

"Where is your God now?" I asked quietly.

The question carried more sorrow than anger.

"Where was He when you locked me beneath your house?" I continued. "When you told me love itself was evil?"

Her lips moved, but no sound came out.

Her eyes darted toward my father.

He didn't move.

He simply watched.

I stepped closer until the smoke surrounded us both. "Tell me something," I said gently. "Do I still look possessed to you?"

Then the smoke burst outward.

Hundreds of luminous butterflies spiraled through the air, their wings glowing softly as they drifted upward toward the lanterns. The crowd erupted instantly, rising to their feet with cheers and applause that thundered through the tent.

But my mother didn't move.

She stood there frozen while the butterflies dissolved into fading sparks.

Finally she turned toward my father, her voice thin and shaking. "What is this?" she demanded. "Why is she here? You said—we came to stop this."

My father looked at her quietly.

"I told you I couldn't find her," he said.

Her eyes widened.

"That was a lie."

The words landed heavily between them.

"I brought you here," he continued softly, "because I needed you to see what you did."

Her breath caught.

"You tricked me?" she whispered.

"I needed you to look at her," he said. "Really look. And see what your hatred created."

Around us the crowd began to file out of the tent, their voices rising with excitement and disbelief as they talked about the performance they had just witnessed.

But my mother remained standing beneath the fading lights.

I walked toward her slowly.

The last spotlight followed me, catching in my hair like starlight. Behind me the rest of the circus watched silently, their presence steady and protective.

When I stopped in front of her, she looked up at me with wide, terrified eyes.

Her lips trembled.

"Demon," she whispered.

"I'm not the devil," I said quietly.

The smoke curled lazily around my shoulders.

"But you're right to be afraid."

My voice softened as I continued.

"You taught me prayers like punishment. Made me kneel until my legs bled while you forced me to whisper verses you never lived by. You told me if I repented hard enough, maybe God would forgive me for who I was."

She shook her head weakly.

Denial.

Confusion.

Or perhaps both.

"You believed your faith would save you from the truth," I said gently.

I gestured softly around us.

"But here it is."

Her voice returned at last, thin and desperate.

"Please," she whispered. "If I say the right verse… will this stop?"

I leaned closer, my whisper drifting against her ear like ash.

"Try it."

The Bible trembled violently in her hands.

"See if it works."

Then I straightened.

"You don't get to run tonight," I told her quietly. "You will see me. And you will remember."

For the first time in my life, she had no control over me – I was in charge.

I turned and walked away.

My footsteps echoed softly through the nearly empty tent while the lanterns dimmed one by one behind me.

And when I glanced back once more, my mother still stood there frozen and alone beneath the fading lights—caught forever in the space between revelation and ruin.

Chapter Forty

Under the Big Top

Reflections in the Mirror Tent

After the last of the crowd had drifted out into the cool night and the lanterns outside the big top began to dim, I found my father again.

He stood near the edge of the ring where the sawdust had already begun to settle back into quiet stillness. For a long moment neither of us spoke. We simply watched the same figure standing alone beneath the fading lights.

My mother.

She had not moved since the applause ended. The Bible was clutched tightly in both of her hands now, her knuckles pale against the leather cover. Her eyes were wide and unfocused, darting across the empty tent as if the shadows themselves might rise up to speak to her. Her lips trembled with silent prayers she could no longer quite remember.

"I need to ask you something," I said quietly.

My father turned toward me, the lantern glow catching the tired lines of his face. "Anything."

I hesitated for only a moment before speaking again. "What I'm about to do to her… there's no undoing it. No walking it back once it begins." My voice stayed calm, though something deep inside my chest felt like it was tightening slowly. "Once she steps inside the mirror tent, the glass will show her everything. Not just what happened—but what it felt like. She'll live it all again. Every cruelty. Every moment she inflicted on someone else. She'll experience it as if it's happening to her."

My father didn't answer immediately.

Instead he looked across the ring toward the woman he had once loved, the woman he had once defended even when the truth had stood plainly before him. She looked smaller now somehow, like the weight of the night had finally begun to collapse the brittle certainty she had carried her entire life.

"She's already broken," he said after a long silence. "She just made sure you were the one who carried the pieces."

I studied him carefully. "So you're okay with it?"

His gaze lowered briefly before returning to mine. "I don't know if I'm okay," he admitted softly. "But I won't stop you."

That was enough.

I nodded once and turned toward the shadows beyond the ring. They came forward almost immediately, stepping out of the darkness with quiet purpose. My family. The ones who understood pain not as something that destroyed you, but as something you could rise from if you survived it.

Sabine moved to my left, the faint glow of embers dancing across her fingertips like restless fireflies. Lilith took my other side, her tattooed arms shifting slowly beneath her skin as the ink responded to the tension in the air. Behind them came the rest of the circus— the fire-breathers, the aerialists, the twins who seemed to exist half inside dreams themselves. Madame Thorne stepped forward last, her presence calm and regal as always, though there was something heavy in her eyes tonight.

"Bring her," I said.

No one rushed. No one spoke harshly. They simply moved together, surrounding my mother with a quiet inevitability that left her nowhere to run. She didn't fight them. Her steps were slow and uncertain, like someone moving through the fevered haze of a nightmare she hadn't yet realized she couldn't wake from.

We guided her toward the far side of the circus grounds where the mirror tent waited.

The velvet entrance parted with a soft whisper as we stepped inside.

The air within the tent pulsed with a deep crimson glow, as though the canvas walls themselves held a heartbeat beneath them. The mirrors that lined the interior no longer reflected simple images. Each surface shimmered faintly, as though something inside the glass had begun to wake.

Memory.

My mother stopped in the center of the tent, the Bible still clutched tightly in her trembling hands.

Then the first mirror flickered.

At first the image was faint, like fog gathering across water. But slowly the scene sharpened.

A child stood there.

Small. Shivering.

Me.

My skin was mottled with cold as icy water dripped from my hair. The girl in the mirror trembled violently while another figure dragged her from the bath with rough hands, praying loudly as if the act itself were sacred.

My mother gasped.

The memory continued.

A belt cutting through the air.

The sharp crack of leather against tender skin.

Scripture shouted like a weapon.

Her scream tore from her throat as she doubled forward, clutching her own back as if the lash had struck her instead.

Another mirror ignited.

The darkness of the cellar unfolded across the glass. Rats crawled across the stone floor while the small girl huddled in the corner with her arms wrapped around her knees. Her voice trembled as she tried to repeat the verses forced into her mouth.

"You must repeat the verse!" the voice in the memory demanded. "Say it again! The devil flees when scripture is spoken!"

But the child in the mirror only cried.

Now my mother screamed.

She stumbled backward as the pain surged through her body, clutching at her feet as though unseen teeth were tearing at her skin. The Bible slipped in her grasp as her knees buckled.

Another mirror flared to life.

Her sister appeared within its glass—bloodied, shaking, being dragged toward the door of their home while accusations rained down around her. The memory burned bright and brutal in the reflection.

Every mirror began to glow.

Every cruelty.

Every sin.

And with each one, she felt it.

The belt struck her again.

The rats bit her skin.

The freezing water climbed her limbs until her body trembled violently.

She tried to pray. Tried to scream scripture through chattering teeth. But the words fell apart in her mouth now, twisted into desperate fragments.

The Bible in her hands began to smoke.

Its pages curled and blackened as if something inside the tent rejected it entirely. With a strangled sob she dropped it to the ground, staring wildly at the mirrors closing in around her.

I stepped forward.

My voice was steady when I spoke.

"You believed God made you barren because of what you did to your sister," I said quietly. "You thought that was punishment."

She looked up at me with wide, pleading eyes.

"But that was mercy."

I leaned down until my breath brushed softly against her ear.

"You have no idea what punishment really is."

She collapsed fully to her knees then, clutching her stomach as though the earth itself might open beneath her and swallow her whole. Her gaze darted frantically around the tent, searching for an escape that no longer existed.

Then the air shifted.

The canvas walls trembled slightly as a massive shadow moved across the entrance.

The Beast Tamer stepped inside.

His presence filled the tent like a gathering storm, the darkness around him moving as though it had weight. The mirrors reflected him again and again until his towering form seemed to exist everywhere at once.

"We have seen the beast that lives inside your soul," he said, his voice echoing across the glass.

He raised one hand slowly.

"And now the world will see it too."

The air cracked.

Her scream shattered into a terrible roar.

I watched as the transformation tore through her body. Flesh twisted violently. Bones cracked with wet, splintering sounds that echoed through the tent. Dark fur erupted across her arms while her fingers split apart into claws that scraped wildly across the ground.

Her mouth stretched too wide, teeth sharpening into something monstrous and wrong.

She writhed.

She fought.

But the curse had already taken hold.

The mirrors went dark all at once.

Silence swallowed the tent.

When the crimson glow returned, my mother was gone.

In her place crouched the beast.

Madame Thorne stepped quietly beside me, her expression calm but solemn. "The curse is complete," she said.

I looked into the mirrors again.

My reflection stared back at me—steady, unbroken, finally whole.

"She was never afraid of the devil," I murmured softly.

My gaze drifted toward the creature crouched in the center of the tent.

"She just never imagined he would look like her."

Chapter Forty-One

Under the Big Top

The Morning After

Dawn arrived quietly.

Pale streaks of lavender and soft blue stretched across the sky above the fairgrounds, the early light brushing gently over canvas tents, wagon wheels, and the thin veil of ash that still lingered in the grass. The circus grounds felt strangely muted in the morning calm, like the world itself was holding its breath in the fragile space between endings and beginnings.

I sat just outside the big tent with my legs drawn close to my chest, my chin resting lightly on my knees. The air was cool against my skin, carrying the faint smell of smoke from the dying fire pits scattered around the camp. I had not slept. Not truly. My body had rested in brief, drifting moments of quiet, but my mind had remained awake—turning slowly through the memories of everything that had happened inside the mirror tent.

Behind me, the canvas stood silent.

No screams.

No shimmering reflections.

Only the still echo of what had been done there.

Most of the circus had finally gone to bed sometime before the sky began to lighten. A few performers still lingered near the fire pits, quietly tending to the last glowing embers while the night gave way to morning. Madame Thorne had slipped away hours earlier, retreating to her tent without a word. Sabine and Lilith had stayed beside me for a while after the flames in the mirror tent died, their warmth steady against my sides while we watched the stars slowly fade. When I finally whispered that I needed a little space, they hadn't argued. Sabine had pressed a soft kiss against my temple while Lilith brushed her fingers through my hair, and then they had left me alone with the quiet sky.

The world felt different now.

Not lighter.

But clearer.

The soft crunch of boots on damp grass broke the silence.

I turned my head slightly as my father approached, two small tin mugs balanced carefully in his hands. He offered one to me without speaking, and I accepted it with a small nod. The coffee inside was strong and bitter, the heat of it spreading slowly through my fingers as I wrapped my hands around the cup.

"I couldn't sleep either," he said as he lowered himself beside me.

We sat there together for a while, sipping in silence while the light of morning slowly stretched across the grounds. It was the kind of silence that carried weight—not uncomfortable, but full of things that had not yet found their way into words.

Eventually I spoke.

"I meant what I said last night," I murmured. "There's no going back now."

My father's gaze drifted toward the mirror tent standing in the distance. Even in the morning light it looked darker than the other tents, its canvas heavy with memory.

"I know," he said quietly.

I lowered my eyes to the grass beneath my boots, watching the dew sparkle faintly in the growing sunlight.

"Do you think I'm a monster?"

The question left my mouth softly, barely louder than the breeze moving through the fairgrounds.

He didn't answer right away.

Instead he turned toward me, studying my face in the quiet way only someone who has known you your entire life can. His eyes held something deep and complicated—grief, pride, regret, and something gentler beneath all of it.

"No," he said finally.

His voice was steady.

"I think you survived one."

The words settled between us as he continued.

"And you made sure she couldn't hurt anyone else again."

I nodded slowly, though the weight of it still pressed against my chest.

"She felt everything," I whispered. "Every rat bite. Every lash. Every cruel word she ever used against me. She heard them all the way I did when I was small. I wanted her to understand… but now that it's done…"

My fingers tightened slightly around the mug.

"Is it justice if it hurts this much?"

My father exhaled slowly.

For a long moment he watched the horizon where the sun was beginning to push above the distant trees. When he finally spoke again, his voice carried the quiet gravity of someone who had spent the night asking himself the same question.

"Justice isn't supposed to feel good," he said. "If it did, it would just be revenge wearing a better mask."

He paused, then glanced toward me again.

"But sometimes the two live side by side. And if what you did gave peace to the people she hurt… maybe that's enough."

I closed my eyes briefly, letting the words settle somewhere deep inside me.

Footsteps approached behind us.

Sabine's voice broke the quiet first, calm and warm as always. "We're taking the mirror tent down today."

I turned slightly to see her standing there beside Lilith, the faint glow of morning firelight still flickering in her hair.

"It's done what it was meant to do," she added.

I nodded slowly.

"It doesn't belong in what comes next."

Lilith stepped closer then, her gaze thoughtful as she looked toward the tent. "Neither do the ghosts."

A small breath left my chest.

"Then let's burn them," I said.

The four of us walked together across the quiet fairgrounds toward the mirror tent, the morning light growing brighter with every step. The rest of the circus slowly gathered around us, their movements calm and respectful as if they understood that what we were doing now mattered just as much as what had happened the night before.

Inside the tent, the air still carried the faint metallic scent of magic spent.

Madame Thorne stood waiting near the center, her expression solemn but peaceful. Without a word she raised one gloved hand and touched the nearest mirror.

The glass shattered instantly.

But the shards never reached the ground.

Each piece crumbled into pale dust before it could fall, dissolving into the air like something that had never truly existed. One by one she moved through the tent, touching each mirror in turn until the walls of reflections collapsed into drifting clouds of silver powder.

When the last one fell away, Sabine stepped forward.

She tossed a torch into the center of the empty space.

The fire that bloomed from it burned violet instead of gold, spreading across the canvas walls with slow, hungry grace. The remaining fragments of silver glass melted instantly as the flames consumed them.

I stood there watching it burn.

The memories.

The cruelty.

The shadows that had followed me for so many years.

I didn't cry.

I didn't speak.

I simply watched until the flames died down and the tent collapsed into nothing but smoke and pale ash drifting into the morning sky.

When it was finished, I turned away.

And this time, I didn't look back.

The past was ashes now.

And I finally had something new to build.

Chapter Forty-Two

Under the Big Top

A New Act Begins

Word spread through the town faster than any traveling circus ever could.

By morning, every alley, every parlor, every church pew hummed with whispers of the same name. It moved from mouth to mouth like a spark catching dry kindling.

Evelyn Ashmoor.

The girl who vanished.
The girl who returned.
The girl who became something more.

Some called me a witch. Others called me brave. Most simply didn't know what to call me at all.

The town itself had not changed very much. The same crooked streets ran between the same rows of wooden storefronts. The same church bell rang out every hour like a heartbeat echoing across the valley. The same gossip drifted from porch to porch the way it always had.

But I had changed.

And I was no longer hiding.

I stepped into the daylight with my head held high, the velvet cloak around my shoulders catching softly in the morning breeze. Smoke-dark eyeliner framed my eyes, and the quiet confidence in my stride seemed to ripple through the streets ahead of me like a silent declaration.

Lilith walked beside me, her tattooed arms bare in the sunlight, the ink beneath her skin shifting faintly like living constellations. Sabine took my other side, a small flicker of flame dancing lazily between her fingertips as if it were simply another extension of her breath.

None of us spoke.

We didn't need to.

The streets fell quiet as we passed.

People paused in their doorways. Conversations stopped halfway through sentences. Shopkeepers leaned against their counters, watching through dusty glass windows as we walked by like something pulled from a story they had never believed could be real.

A small girl standing near the edge of the road gasped softly when she saw us. Her eyes widened, sparkling with something like awe. After a moment she raised her hand and waved.

I smiled and waved back.

Across the street, a shopkeeper watched with narrowed eyes, his fingers hovering uncertainly over the rosary hanging beside the register.

An older man shuffled out of the hardware store just as we passed. His back was hunched with age, his eyes blinking slowly behind thick spectacles as he studied my face.

"I remember you," he murmured quietly. "You were just a child."

I nodded.

"I still am," I said softly. "And I'm also not."

He stared at me for a moment, clearly unsure what to make of the answer, but after a pause he tipped his hat anyway.

Not everyone kept their distance.

Some people followed.

They trailed behind us with cautious curiosity, whispering quietly to one another. A few gathered the courage to step forward, offering quiet words of thanks they didn't quite know how to shape.

For surviving.

For returning.

For refusing to disappear the way so many others had before.

Eventually my steps carried me to the edge of town where the old gravel path wound toward the house I had once called home. The weeds had grown thick along the walkway, and the paint on the porch had begun to peel away in pale, curling strips.

I walked past the house without hesitation and stopped behind it.

The cellar door was still there.

Half hidden beneath creeping vines and warped wooden boards, the rusted latch barely visible beneath years of neglect. For a long moment I simply stared at it, remembering the sound it used to make when it slammed shut behind me.

My hands didn't tremble when I reached down and lifted the latch.

The door creaked open slowly, the sound echoing hollowly down into the darkness below like something ancient waking from sleep.

The air inside was cold and still.

I stepped down the narrow stairs alone.

The cellar had changed more than the house above it. The chains were gone. The narrow cot had been removed. Even the torn pages of scripture that once clung to the damp stone walls had vanished.

Only the stone remained.

Silent.

Empty.

I stood there for a moment, breathing slowly, letting the quiet settle around me without fear.

Then I turned and climbed back up the stairs.

When I stepped outside again, I left the cellar door wide open behind me.

Some places no longer need to be buried.

That night the circus tent filled once more.

But the energy inside it had changed.

The crowd no longer gathered out of shock or morbid fascination. Something quieter moved through the air now—something closer to reverence mixed with curiosity. Word had spread across the town faster than the posters or the rumors ever could.

The Girl in Smoke had returned.

When I stepped into the ring, I wore no mask.

There was no illusion of vengeance lingering in the air, no shadow of the confrontation that had taken place beneath the tent the night before.

There was only me.

The music began to swell slowly through the canvas walls, low strings rising into a steady rhythm that pulsed through the sawdust beneath my feet. The fog curled up around my ankles as it always had, but tonight it felt different.

Not like chains.

Like wings.

When the smoke lifted me gently from the ground, I didn't rise to escape.

I rose to fly.

My body moved through the air in long, sweeping arcs of light and shadow, every movement unfolding like a story told without words. The fog bent and twisted around me as though it understood the rhythm of my breath. Each turn, each spiral, each quiet moment of stillness carried something deeper than performance.

It was reclamation.

They watched in silence.

Not as if they were witnessing a spectacle.

But as if they were finally seeing me.

Not a monster.

Not a sinner.

Not even the girl who had once been broken.

Just Evelyn.

Fire blossomed behind me as Sabine stepped into the ring, her flames rising and falling like a heartbeat. Lilith followed close behind, her inked arms lifting toward the lantern light as constellations of glowing shapes formed in the air above us.

Together we moved through the performance like three threads woven into the same living tapestry.

We were not simply entertaining them.

We were surviving out loud.

When the final flare of flame died away and the smoke slowly settled across the ring, I stood at the center of it all with my arms lifted toward the open sky above the tent.

The applause began softly.

Then it grew.

And grew.

Until the entire tent thundered with the sound.

But I didn't need it anymore.

Because tonight the act wasn't for them.

It was for me.

Chapter Forty-Three

Under the Big Top

The Road Ahead

The camp quieted slowly as the sun dipped behind the trees, painting the fairgrounds in long streaks of gold and amber. The applause from the evening performance had faded hours ago, leaving behind only the gentle rustle of canvas and the creak of wagon wheels being prepared for travel. One by one, the townspeople had drifted back to their homes, their minds filled with smoke and spectacle and the lingering echo of something they would struggle to explain for the rest of their lives.

Now only the circus remained.

Performers moved through the clearing with quiet efficiency, folding canvas, coiling ropes, securing lanterns and props into the backs of painted wagons. The great striped tent that had dominated the town square all week was already half lowered, its towering poles slowly coming down like the careful closing of some enormous, watchful eye.

The circus was moving on.

At the edge of the clearing, Madame Thorne stood with her face turned toward the wind. Her dark coat stirred softly around her ankles as she listened to something no one else could hear. She didn't speak, but I had begun to understand the way her silence worked. It wasn't empty. It was listening.

Somewhere out there, another soul was hurting.

Another town was holding its breath beneath the weight of secrets.

The call always came.

And we would always answer.

Near the center of the clearing, a small fire burned low in the pit where we had gathered so many nights before. The flames were smaller now, their light softer, flickering gently across the faces of the performers gathered around it. There were quiet conversations drifting through the air, small bursts of laughter, and the occasional hush of emotion that came when people understood they were about to part ways with a place they had briefly called home.

Eventually my attention drifted toward the far edge of the clearing where my father stood. He had remained just outside the circle of performers all evening, watching quietly while the camp prepared to move again. His shoulders were squared in that familiar way he had when he was trying to appear stronger than he felt, his hands tucked into the pockets of his coat.

I walked toward him slowly.

"You don't have to stay here," I said gently when I reached him. "There's a place for you with us if you want it."

He studied me for a long moment before answering.

"I did terrible things," he said quietly. "Not by raising my hand… but by standing still when I should have stopped someone else's." His gaze drifted briefly toward the distant shape of the house barely visible beyond the trees. "And still you let me back in. You gave me a second chance."

"You earned it," I said. "But what you do with it now… that part is yours."

He nodded slowly.

For a moment his eyes lingered on the road leading back toward town, toward the porch light that still burned faintly in the distance.

"This town might never forget who I was," he admitted. "But maybe that's alright. Maybe remembering is part of the work." He took a slow breath before continuing. "Maybe I can make that house something better than it ever was before. Something good."

"You can," I said softly.

He looked back at me then, the guilt in his eyes seeming lighter.

"And if you ever want to find us again," I added, "you'll know how."

We didn't say goodbye.

Not really.

Because even as we stepped apart, both of us understood something that would have seemed impossible once.

Distance no longer meant the same thing it used to.

Not now.

Not for me.

I wasn't the girl who had been trapped in a cellar beneath a house full of scripture and silence.

I wasn't a ghost made only of smoke and pain.

I was something else entirely now.

Wind and flame and shadow.

A girl forged in fire who had chosen to rise.

Behind me, the wagons began to move.

The wooden wheels creaked softly as they rolled forward across the grass, lanterns swaying gently from their hooks. Performers climbed into their places while ropes were tightened and horses guided carefully onto the road.

The last of the tent poles came down, the canvas folding inward like the slow blink of a sleeping giant.

Madame Thorne lifted her cane.

The camp stirred instantly to life.

I didn't look back.

Instead I stepped forward onto the road waiting beyond the clearing, the soft glow of the caravan lanterns stretching ahead of me into the gathering dusk.

Not running.

Not proving anything.

Just following the call of something older and larger than the life I had left behind.

The road was calling now.

And this time, I was ready.